LADY VENOM TAKES A MISTRESS

KAT BLACKTHORNE

Dear Darling Reader,

This is the story of Poesy Laroche finding her lady. It is not a history book or intended to be historical fiction. This takes place sometime in the far past, in the Halloween Boys (Kat Blackthorne) universe. Thorneverse? If corsets worn with fishnet stockings, mixed with old gothic vibes, but there's still running water, aren't your thing, she's probably not the lady for you. For everyone else... This is a we're here and we're queer world and nothing less than acceptance for love exists in the Thorneverse.

Welcome to an aggressively sapphic tale. Triggers include but are not limited to: SA, gore, graphic murder, violence, blood, dubcon, and snakes... like a lot of snakes. Check my author site for a full content list.

Now, step into my forest, get lost in my maze, and be a good girl and turn the page.

Xoxo,
Kat

PROLOGUE

"The stories aren't true. The stories aren't true," he whimpered as he heaved and slammed up against the briars of the maze. A thick fog had encompassed the space, a dense cloud of gloom beneath the looming gothic manor. George Gregory had come to find the evil entity himself. *I'll find her, have my way with her, and drag her back to town and show you all there's nothing to fear in these woods.* My, how wrong Mr. Gregory had been. Had he passed that turn before? The ivy all looked the same, and around every bend, the fear of what he might find gripped his chest. George's bearded face snagged against a thorn, but despite the blood, he couldn't stop, because something flung itself from the earth below him. A scream of terror and pain gurgled from his throat as he shook his ankle, running forward and falling. Pain throbbed like lightning bolts of agony up his spine, and he began to shake. The sound of hissing and rattling vibrated around him as a pair of pointed black shoes appeared at his nose. He strained as the poison wormed its way into his heart. A red snake slithered over the boot and struck his face.

And that is how Lady Venom's fourth murder of that year took place.

The stories were indeed true.

CHAPTER ONE

Lady Venom always killed seven men a year. Some said her poisons lured them through the woods and onto her estate, where they slowly went mad. Others claimed the men who went searching for her wandered for eternity in the maze in front of her castle. If you were very quiet and very still, on some winter nights, rumor was you could hear their screams of torment. Lady Venom was what you spoke about with passersby when you had nothing else to say. If your house cat wandered into the woods, no one would dare fetch it. We'd say, "Oh, it belongs to Lady Venom now." What she did to the creatures that wandered into her lair, I didn't want to think about.

But thinking after Lady Venom was a distraction from the terror of my own life. Today was the day I'd been dreading since it had come about last year. My mother checked the pockets of my petticoat, combed my ringlet blond curls, and pressed my only nice dress. Well, the only dress I hadn't destroyed in blood or fire or cow manure.

"You're not disgracing us at this bidding, Poesy ," she said, tying the long pink satin ribbon around my neck. She held the long end and assessed me. "I dare say we'll get a great many bids. Chin up, dear. This is an honor."

Little did my mother know that I still had a trick up my sleeve. "You're right," I lied. "I'll behave."

I followed behind her, attached to the string, the ribbon that meant so much more than a symbolic leash. My life, my freedom, my future, were at the mercy of the highest bidder. Other girls filtered into town, shuffling alongside me.

Zalia pushed her way through the crowd, her green ribbon dragging behind her, and locked her arm with mine. "Another year, another bidding. What's the plan this time?"

I hushed her while checking to ensure my mother was lost in chatter with the other women as we forged ahead to the middle of town square. "Not all of us can be blessed with short stature," I playfully nudged my friend, who giggled in response.

"It's not my fault no one wants a short wife. Though it certainly does work to my benefit." She gathered up her ribbon and twirled it. "Mother doesn't even care to put on the display anymore. I crocheted all day."

I groaned. "Quit bragging. I had to soak in tea for four hours before squeezing into this ridiculous little thing."

"Well, I can't wait to see what you pull out of your hat." She laughed. "It's always such fun watching the men's horrified expressions."

I put a gloved hand to my mouth. "I do love horrifying men."

"Ladies," a prim voice interrupted. "Stop the unsavory talk, or one might think you're destined to be as haggard and destitute as Lady Venom."

Zalia shuddered. "Don't even mention the name. I swear I heard men's screams coming from the forest a few nights ago."

"And the hissing," I reminded. "Of all the ssssnakes."

Opaline, our redheaded proper friend, rolled her eyes. "If either of you would take this seriously, you might catch a bid for once."

Zalia raised a dark eyebrow. "So we can be as happy as you?"

"I am happy. I am under my husband's care. I want for nothing," Opaline said without conviction. I lightly kicked my loud-mouthed friend's shin, urging her to stop the teasing. If Opaline was lying to herself, we shouldn't intervene. Opal had been the attraction of the town three years ago. Her very first bidding made town history as the highest bid of all time. Nearly twenty men had fought for her hand. Unfortunately, the winner's virtue was not as full as his wallet. He was also old, very old, so I guessed that worked in my friend's favor. We could only silently hope he would die, leaving her in peace.

To be won in a bid was to be a slave. The delicate ribbons around our necks were physical mockeries of our chains. Being roped like cattle and sold by our parents to men who came from all over in search of a bride. Men got a young lady who had been trained from birth to do his bidding, have his babies, clean his house, bear his lashings. And our parents, my mother, depending on the bid, got a handsome sum of money. It was horrid, but it was our lot in life. The best we could hope for was a rich man with a weak arm.

The collective chatter silenced as we neared the round city square. Men in top hats and canes smoked pipes and guffawed as we approached. There were a dozen of us girls this year. New ones who'd just reached eighteen and old ones like Zalia and me, who were deemed defective year after year. Zalia's was due to her height, and I envied her being born with a god-given gift of tininess. I had to be more creative in my attempts to deter the men and avoid being bought.

Zalia's mother appeared and straightened her daughter's collar before taking hold of the green ribbon and joining my mother. My friend gave my hand a squeeze. "As always, let's hope to be the ugliest."

"Or for a rich old man with a bad cough." I forced a smile, repeating the slogan we'd repeated for four years now. Each year, the terror was the same. How many tricks did I have? How much longer until I looked too old to be bought? My hair had already grown past my shoulders from where I shaved it on my eighteenth year. My mother had been so furious she didn't feed me supper for a week.

Shears had disappeared from our modest little shack then and had never returned. I'd resorted to destroying my gowns instead, and last year, I'd rolled in poison ivy, bringing about a horridly itchy rash. But it scared off the bidders. In my mother's industrious style, she acquired a goat who ate all the ivy and waited until this morning to buy my gown from a seamstress. But I still had my schemes. I wouldn't be handed over to some nasty bald man without a fight.

Sometimes I wished I could be as compliant as Opaline. She'd accepted her fate, and instead of fighting against it, she fought to find the best in it, to make the best of it. But I couldn't do the same, no matter how hard I wrestled with the thought. I wasn't sure what I was supposed to feel in the presence of a suitor who wanted to wed me, but I'd never felt anything but disdain and repulsion at the men who came seeking brides.

My mother tugged my leash before centering me in the middle of the row of girls. She fluffed my pink gown and took a step back as the men gathered. The smell of smoke and sweat haunted my nightmares, along with their roaming eyes. One gray haired grandpa started with the girl next to me, instructing her to open her mouth. She did as she was told, and he tugged at her teeth. Several passed by

Zalia, who was at the end of the row. Lucky. Three stopped to look at me, and I avoided eye contact.

"Can she milk a cow?" one asked my mother, who eagerly said that I could. He didn't seem impressed as he continued down the line.

My mother lingered, whispering over my shoulder. "Don't mind him. He's not the one we're after. I heard rumor that Lord Harkness would be here, and it seems his carriage just arrived." She sucked in a breath. "Oh, happy day, Poesy. Could it be the gods have given me such a foolish child to finally reward me for my labors?"

My mother's insults no longer stung. In fact, they didn't land at all. The only thing that mattered was surviving another year. The twenty or so men stepped back into a line across from us after the assessment phase. The announcer called the first girl, and men began to bid.

"Four pounds!"

"Four and a half!" And onward until her ribbon was handed to a man with a limp and warts. Her head drooped as she followed after him.

Zalia's eyes met mine in worry when the announcer called my name.

"Poesy Laroche, age twenty-two."

A man in a top hat and monocle started the bid at three, and my heart sank. However, my mother clapped. "Smile, dear," she encouraged.

"Yes, Mother," I obliged, finding the smile coming easily while the men gawked. Quickly, I bit at the lining I'd sewn under my white glove, releasing the black powder. After swirling it along my teeth,

I smiled broadly. The men's faces dropped, and the one who'd bid quickly rescinded his offer.

"What have you done?" my mother scolded when she saw my black smile.

I shrugged. "Sorry, Mother, but it's my life, not yours."

Zalia couldn't contain her giggle as the announcer moved on to the next girl. A wave of relief relaxed my shoulders as my mother started sniffling her tears behind me.

"Oh, why have the gods cursed me with this wretched child?" she moaned.

And then a man approached. Around me, the gentlemen fell silent, and the bidding stopped. His cape was bright red, and his walk reminded me of the rooster in our coop. Though he wasn't old. Maybe forty years. And he was strong, with his chin high in the air as he walked the line, stalling the festivities.

"Lord Harkness, welcome," the announcer finally stated. "As is customary, it is our honor to offer you your pick of the bunch, despite previous biddings."

Men shifted and puffed around us as I shoved at my mother to stop touching my face and fluffing my curls. The Lord looked down his nose at each girl, passing by even the most beautiful ones. The men who'd bid already sighed audibly in relief as he disregarded their winnings. And then he was next to me. His eyes flicked from the girl beside me, to my dress, then to my eyes. He cocked his head. "Name?"

I made to respond and show him my inky surprise when my mother cut in. "Poesy Laroche, my lord."

He reached out, tugging my hips, and my discomfort burned at the intrusion. "Nice wide hips for bearing children. Solid shoulders and jaw. Though I'm not keen on the faded redness of her hair…"

"It grows blonder in the sunlight," my mother quacked like a duck behind me. I wished I could kick her and this puffed-up Lord Harkness and run away.

He hummed, scratching his cleft chin. He was so close I could smell his nauseating scent of cigars and beer. Without looking at my mother, he asked, "Can you assure me she bears sons only? I'd like six strapping boys."

Kill me.

My mother's delight was evident and stupefying in her tone. "Absolutely. We have tonics for that, and she's been taking them in her porridge for years."

I had no idea if that was true or not. It likely was. Even more likely, though, was that my mother would say anything to get me a bid. And to secure this smelly lord would mean a sizable bounty for her on top of the bonus of not having to care for me anymore. My reward? Becoming a baby factory. Fun.

"Well, don't look so downtrodden. I may just bid on you yet," Lord Harkness chided, and chuckles followed after him. It wasn't funny, and I wasn't in the habit of laughing at jokes that weren't humorous, but I smiled anyway. Big and broad, letting all the saliva I'd held in my cheeks spill down my chin. A woman gasped in horror, and girls covered their mouths with lacy gloves. My mother gasped, trying to pull me backward. But Lord Harkness only grabbed my arm harshly, furrowing his brow at my black mouth. It went quiet, everyone waiting to see what he'd do. Would he strike me? Walk away disgusted? A beating was surely awaiting me when I arrived home.

And then I jumped as he tilted his chin to the sky and let out a bellow of a laugh. With that, the other men laughed as well, doubling over at my state. I felt nothing but hope that this would deter him, and them, from wanting me. The charcoal had done its job.

But then, as the lord dried his eyes with a handkerchief from his breast pocket, he turned on his heel. "Her, I'm taking her."

And that's how my entire world fell apart.

CHAPTER TWO

Days passed in a flurry of tulle and sadness. I hadn't seen Lord Harkness at all, despite his swift insistence that we marry as quickly as possible. We wouldn't be getting married on his estate, my new cage—I mean home. We'd be married here on my tiny farm. My mother cried in happiness at the bounty she'd receive and at knowing she was finally free of me. The Lord's men set up tents all over the farm while my mother and her friends began setting up the wedding venue. Fluffy, white, sickeningly sweet flowers were bundled everywhere. I hated the smell of them. I hated how happy my mother was. I hated that my last trick to get out of the bidding had failed. And worse, that it had maybe even enticed Lord Harkness further. He thought my stubbornness would breed strong sons, and my mother assured him over and over that it would. The grassy hill that led to an archway of white flowers may as well have been a guillotine. That would've been a mercy death and would've been much kinder than any man in my world.

My friends comforted me by saying that because Lord Harkness was an important man, that he'd often be gone on his travels. Then I would have his home and land and staff all to myself. They told me that I should be grateful I'd been chosen by such a powerful man. Because really, that's the best that I could hope for with my life, wasn't it? To be chosen by some man. To be used, filled with children, and worked around his estate. To die alone and miserable, having never done anything I wanted to do. What did I want to do? I'd never had much of a chance to think about it. Most of my upbringing had been spent thinking about the bidding and how to avoid the bidding and mourning for my friends who had been bought. What would life be like if I'd had the luxury of thinking of such things? A life where I had time to be bored and figure out what I wanted to do, who I wanted to be. I couldn't imagine such a thing. But I did know that of all the brief imaginings I was afforded, none of them ever included a man, least of all Lord Harkness.

The night before my hanging—I mean wedding—I snuck out of my room, letting the pads of my feet touch the cold grass outside. I went to the chicken coop and stroked the feathers of my favorite hen, Marcy, while a fire crackled in the distance and men drunkenly laughed and shared stories. All of a sudden, a startle shook through me as a grizzly scream echoed through the forest beyond my farm. The men stood, looking at each other, and then looked toward the woods when another scream pierced through the dead of night. My heart caught in my chest. I knew that scream. I knew those screams. They had become my lullaby these last several years. Drifting to sleep to the sounds of men dying at the hand of some hideous, villainess woman in the woods. The legend, a force, something deadly and terrible.

The men looked at each other, paling and grabbing their shotguns. "You go look for him," one said.

"Why me? I don't fancy meeting Lady Venom and becoming one of her ghosts tonight, do you? You go. He's your friend."

The men bickered back and forth until something grabbed my shoulder, startling me. A croaky chuckle sounded behind me, and my stomach dropped. "No need to be frightened, my bride. I'm here to protect you," Lord Harkness said with a hiccup. He smelled strongly of alcohol, the smell burning my nose.

I backed away, but his grip only tightened. "No wife of mine should be wandering alone in the night in nothing but her nightgown." He grabbed a hateful bundle of fabric around my hip, the contact worse than a bee sting. "Would you like to have sex with me? Silly question. Of course you would. I imagine a girl like you never expected to be the one chosen by a lord. You must be swimming in gratitude and girlish thoughts." He pinched my cheeks together painfully. "Less honorable men may think you available for their pleasure seeking, out looking like a whore. But no." He hiccuped again, looking sweaty and grotesque in the pale flicker of lantern light. "You are my property, and I'll have you a virgin on our wedding night. Though there are things I could take from you that don't wholly compromise what you're to give me soon..."

My scream was muffled by his sharp and prickly mouth. The stubble of his coarse and unkempt beard clawed at my face like an animal trying to eat me. My first kiss, I thought, was more of a mauling. With all my might, I tried to push him off, but he only grabbed my wrist, pushing a hand between us and scraping up my thigh. "You know why I bid on you over all the much finer girls?" he gruffed, his breath putrid as he pressed me against the splintered chicken coop.

"Get off me," I pleaded helplessly.

His hand cupped my sex harshly as he continued. "I picked you because I could sense the same wild nature as a stallion. Among training all manner of foul and beasts, I'm an expert horseman, which I'm sure you already know. You... Poesy... only need to be broken. And, ah, how I'll enjoy every moment of my breaking you. Hoping your strength passes to my sons. Men who can make use of such things women don't need."

I yelped again as his grip fled to my hair and yanked, pushing me onto my knees. "Go on, stupid girl," he ordered, pulling a flask from his pocket and taking a swig before loosening his trousers and shoving them down. His ugly half-limp cock stared at me like some deranged worm, and I could think of nothing less desirable on this earth.

Looking up at him as he wobbled, I figured if I was going to be forced into this marriage, I'd better get used to it. And maybe he would break me eventually, but not tonight. Not as another scream pierced through the forest. This one sounded garbled, as if the man was choking on his own blood. Lord Harkness shot a concerted stare into the woods.

I willed my voice to sound less afraid. "Some stories say that Lady Venom eats the men she kills. Others say she feeds them to her snakes. I do wonder what man's flesh tastes like." I licked my teeth and eyed his cock.

The Lord's brow furrowed as he placed a moist palm on my face and pushed me backward into a pile of hay and feathers. "You will learn to heed my orders, you disturbed little child. For now, I must aid my men." He knelt, grabbing the front of my gown and hurling me forward so his hot, rancid breath was on my face, making me wince. "I'm going to fuck every hole of yours until you bleed tomorrow night. Do you understand? The moment we're married, you'll never refuse me again."

Throwing me backward, he stood, securing his belt and leaving me in a pile of chicken shit. He was off to contend with the monstrous woman in the woods while I was awaiting sacrifice to a monster far worse. I feared Lady Venom, as everyone did. But I had a secret, too. One I wouldn't dare share with anyone in my dreary little town. The woman of mystery was formidable, feared to the point of mythological proportions. To come near her meant sure and certain death. And I envied her.

CHAPTER THREE

A COUSTICS TREMBLED DOWN THE path to the guillotine as my mother fluffed my outrageous creampuff dress. "I look like a goose," I grumbled as she tied a thick pink bow around my neck. My collar, my leash, my cattle chain.

"You look fit for a lord." She preened. "He will be so pleased when he sees you."

I hated that. I wished to tangle my hair, blister my skin, and wear dirty potato sacks for all of time so men like him would never glance at me twice again. Maybe that's what I should have done to avoid this union. Maybe I was too cowardly to harm myself. But this fate was sure and certain death. I knew my impending husband would make good on his threats of sexing me until I bled and cried for mercy. A fate worse than any demise I could imagine. My mother and two of the lord's men helped me onto a white horse, my skirts billowing over the sides. I rubbed the animal's ear softly, wishing I could trade places with the creature but knowing she was this man's property the same as I was. "We are both trapped mares, aren't we?" I asked her tenderly as the attendants let go of her reins and she trotted down the aisle of onlookers to my waiting evil peacock of a future husband.

The whole town had shown to watch my beheading, I mean wedding. Nosy, bored jerks. Why was no one speaking up about how wrong this was? How this was no way to live or end one's life? Why was I doomed simply for being a woman? The groom looked up at me as the priest spoke about love and duty. It may as well have been a reading of my final job description. Leaning in, the lord patted the horse on its snout. "See, Poesy? All it takes is a few beatings and fuckings, and you'll be as helpless and docile as Penny here."

Penny. Even her name was similar to mine. And for some reason, imagining her beaten, her white fur marred with blood at his hands, lit something inside me. Something like rage, a feeling I'd scarcely allowed myself to truly embody. Trapped, caged animals with nowhere to go, nowhere safe from the men who hunted and captured us. A crow called from the forest beyond, pulling my attention. Nowhere to go except...

I leaned forward and whispered in Penny's ear. "Risk it all with me, please?" I begged her, not sure if horses understood humans or how loyal she was to her lord, regardless. When Harkness and the priest bowed their heads to pray, I gave her reins a yank to the left and kicked her side in the way I'd seen the lord's men do, not knowing if it would work.

But it did.

The mare took off in a gallop so strong, so forceful, I slid back and had to lurch forward to hug her neck for balance. Commotion stirred behind us, but I held on for dear life as the horse darted into the forest, quickly finding a trail, as if she'd been planning this escape, too. Tears of awe and fear streaked my face as leaves and branches cut against my exposed arms. I didn't care. Every gallop forward was farther away from them, from him, from all of that. Men hollered behind us, and I looked over my shoulder, hearing hooves hitting the ground. "Faster, please," I begged Penny, and she obeyed. Jumping over logs and tree roots, she propelled us forward with a speed I didn't know possible.

And I thought maybe I'd done it, maybe I'd finally escaped, but then the forest grew dark. It was midday, but a sort of twilight blue fell over the woods, and a chill in the air made goose bumps stand on my arms. Even Penny slowed to a trot and huffed as she glanced around, sensing something, sensing—

A snake dropped from a tree. Then another, and another, hissing and slithering along the ground. Penny reared back, and I slipped this time, falling onto the forest floor as the rattles and hisses intensified. The horse took off, and I grabbed my skirts, fighting my terror and running after her. That was when I saw it. A manor, a looming gray estate adorned in black.

I jumped over a thick branch. "It's just a branch. It's just a branch that moves," I chanted to myself, panicked, shaking, as I ran toward the only sign of civilization I'd seen. The thought didn't cross my mind that it was hers. Her home. Or maybe it did, and I decided I'd rather die by her hand than by the hand of a man. It didn't matter as I jumped over another *branch* and barreled forward, finding the opening in the thicket, with pathways carved in stone below it. I stopped a moment and took a right, out of breath and panting, still clutching my stupid goose dress. The shrubbery was fragrant, and deep purple lilies and ivy dropped over the sides. I would have stopped to admire them if there weren't so many *snakes*. *Not branches.* There were red striped snakes, serpents with faces like triangles and slits for eyes that stared at me as they slithered along the ground and crowded in bundles in the corners of the maze. That's what it was, a maze, and I was lost in it. Trapped. And then a sound worse than the hissing and rattles came. Men. Someone was shouting behind me. It sounded as if they'd abandoned their horses as well. I glanced over my shoulder, crying now, sobbing and pleading with any universal force—any god or devil that would listen—to please, please help me. In my panic, I tripped over my skirt and fell forward. Only instead of crashing to the ground, I was caught by a set of arms, and my cheek pressed against a soft chest. The smell of cherries instantly warmed my belly before I realized I was in the arms of a woman holding me upright. She gripped my elbows and helped me to stand before cupping my jaw.

"Who did this to you?" she asked, her voice like that of a dark angel. "Tell me who I must kill next."

Trembling in her hold, I couldn't speak. Not from fear or the run. No, her beauty knocked me back harder than the fall from the horse. She was stunning. Her long black hair fell down her milky white shoulders. No, not black, because in the tiny glimmers of sunlight it shone with a dark purple tint. God, purple was my favorite color. No, no, it wasn't. The color of her pale blue eyes was my favorite color now. No, the shade of her perfect ebony painted lips... "Stand behind me," she coaxed gently, helping me to get behind her. "And close your eyes if you fear blood."

I was, in fact, afraid of blood, but I couldn't close my eyes. It was as if I'd stumbled into an eerie dream and was meeting with my own personal gorgeous night terror. Two men strode forward, holding their shotguns steady. "Give us the girl, and we'll leave you be, witch. She is the property of Lord Harkness."

The woman crossed her arms and clicked her tongue, not at all concerned with the guns pointed at her head. "Oh, boys. A woman isn't property at all, and nor are you ignorant fools. Though..." She walked forward, and I gawked at her nerve as she ran a finger down the shaft of the firearm.

"Get back!" one man yelled.

The other glanced over, raising an eyebrow. "Maybe she wants to give us a little fun before we leave?"

Their eyes roamed her curves as greedily as mine had as her long skintight black gown trailed behind her. "Mmm. You will each make the most delicious meal."

"Come have a taste," one replied, lowering his weapon.

"I'm afraid I've already eaten," she purred in his ear before turning to the other, "but they haven't." With a movement so quick I hardly registered it, the woman wielded two knives I hadn't noticed her holding and slit both of their throats at the same time. "Oh, my babies do love when the meat is coated in a little sauce. Makes for swifter swallowing, you see."

The men dropped to their knees, holding their necks. She hadn't cut them deep enough to kill. Only to bleed. And as she turned, four enormous snakes glided out from under the brush of the maze. I gasped as one wrapped around a bleeding man and the other snake struck his companion, causing the man to gurgle out a scream. They were being swallowed whole as they bled out.

The woman turned on her heel, the corner of her mouth lifting slightly as a small splatter of blood stained her cheek like tiny red freckles on her otherwise lily clear skin. "Only the brave or the stupid make it to me. Which are you?"

"Who—who are you?" I stammered out as she prowled toward me like a jungle cat.

"I am Lady Venom, and you, my dear, are now my mistress."

CHAPTER FOUR

I heard voices but didn't see the source as Lady Venom breezed by me.

"What number was that?" the voice whispered.

"That depends if you count it as one or two men."

"Of course it was two men, dimwit."

I was losing my mind and hearing voices in my head when I spotted Lady Venom turn at the top of the stairs and cross her arms. "Zero. The snakes killed them, not me. I only added a little seasoning to their supper."

Who was she talking to? And then I caught a shimmer, like a pearl in the sunlight, of a flowy translucent figure. My hand shot to my mouth to cover my scream, and two ghosts and one Lady Venom remembered my presence. "S-snakes and-and g-ghosts," I stuttered out roughly.

One ghost seemed to put their hand on their hip. "Yes, and what are you? Some sort of bell of the ball? That dress is hideous." She materialized a bit more then, and I could make out the body of a female in a plain white frock.

"Mind your manners, Edith. That's our lady's new mistress." A translucent bald man with tiny glasses materialized. My heart was racing and my head pounding. Surely I was hallucinating. This was a mirage or a fever dream, or I'd hit my head on the way in.

Lady Venom waved a delicate hand. "Darling, pay them no mind, but tell them no secrets. They will show you to your room."

She turned, and I tripped over my muddy skirt as I stepped up the stone stairs to call after her. "Wait, my room? I appreciate that, miss, but I couldn't possibly stay overnight." I glanced around at the various black and purple flowers that seemed to be watching me, and among them, the dozens and dozens of slitted eyes of snakes in all colors of the rainbow. I shuddered, feeling my skin crawl. And then, then, there were the literal ghosts, looking on with hazy gray eyes. Yes, I'd wanted to escape my wretched fate, but not to stay in a haunted, poisonous den of vipers with the deadly witch of the woods herself.

The beautiful woman sighed before slowly clipping down the stairs as if carried on air. How someone could be so dark yet so feminine and deadly, all at once, confounded me. And the sensation that fluttered in my lower belly when she took my chin between her fingers sent thrills of heat between my thighs. Heat like I'd never experienced before as I gazed into her pale blue eyes. "You aren't staying the night, little bellflower."

I breathed a sigh of both relief and slight disappointment. Because despite the horrors of this place, I wouldn't have minded spending a little more time with her. She was possibly the least deadly thing about this place. But then... then she smiled. Wicked and gleaming with two pointed incisors. "You're staying forever. You are mine."

She twirled away, her long eggplant dark hair hitting my chest as she disappeared into the gloomy manor. The two ghosts were by my side, ushering me to follow them inside. Their grips were tight on my arm, holding me up. "You're ghosts," I breathed, my knees feeling weaker by the moment.

"Yes, and you're stinky," Edith quipped, holding her nose. It was hard to tell with how translucent she was, but I believed her to be blond, with her hair tied up in a tight bun.

"I'm Paul. Don't mind my wife. She's only feisty until she gets to know you." The portly older gentleman was wearing suspenders and a bowtie as he walked me inside.

"I'm Poesy," I replied weakly. "Poesy Laroche." I half expected skeletons and rats to jump out at me, but instead, the inside of the massive mansion was dim and floral, in the deepest and coziest of ways. Like the way the sunset pours across a field of wildflowers. The walls were covered in bright green and shining ivy, and it hung from the ceilings in ribbons of green and light purple blooms. The furnishings were black and silver, with artwork peppering the walls and black taper candles burning in every chandelier and dark crevice. The ghosts led me up a spiral staircase and down a long hall. At the end was my room. When they'd shown me, I thought they were surely joking. "All this for me?" I breathed, taking in the space.

"I said the same," Edith sighed, floating over to the large window that overlooked the maze and sprawling estate. "I do love this room."

Paul pulled out several plush blankets from a cabinet and placed them on the foot of the bed. "This and the fireplace should keep you plenty warm. There's running hot water in your washroom anytime you want it. And dinner's at seven in the dining room each night."

"Lady Venom can't really be serious, though, right? I'm not staying *forever*… right?"

The ghosts looked at each other and back at me. "You're her mistress now," Edith said plainly. "Better start acting like it."

Paul elbowed his wife, and she swatted his arm. "Well, let us know if you need anything, Miss Laroche."

"Please call me Poesy," I replied as they floated through the door. "And thank you," I whispered after them. I was sure I'd gone from the guillotine into the mouth of a bear, but I had a warm bed that I wouldn't have to share with Lord Harkness tonight. I was not his bride, at least not until he found me. Though I felt I was far from safe within Lady Venom's grasp, I was at least sheltered and far away from that fate. Even if I'd now slipped straight into a more wicked a deadly end. Perhaps with Lady Venom, that end would not be as swift or as bad. Perhaps I'd get to speak to her more... perhaps... perhaps.

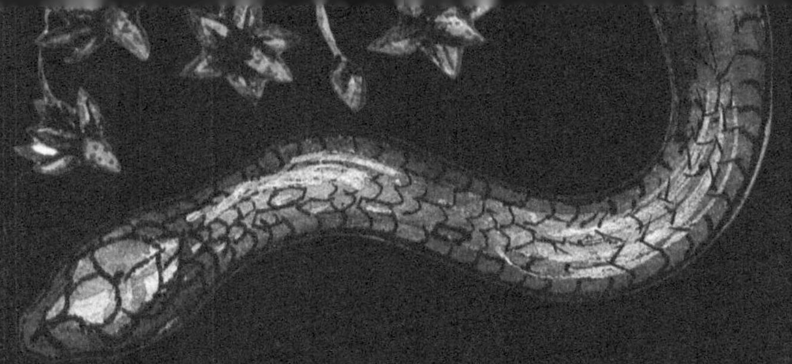

CHAPTER FIVE

Light filtered in through the velvet red drapes, and I awoke to the smell of fresh croissants and eggs. Slipping out of bed, I shrugged on a housecoat and took my croissant to nibble by the window. It had all been real. The snakes, the ghosts, the failed wedding and dying men, and perhaps the most extraordinary of all, Lady Venom. Lady Venom, who was certainly not a witch. Or if she was, she wasn't the haggard and wart-covered one of campfire stories. No, Lady Venom was a scary tale entirely of her own making, and I was a part of that story now, somehow.

The grounds of the estate were exquisite and marvelously tended yet overgrown. It was as if the caretakers valued the opinion and comfort of the wildlife and plants and trimmed around them, building stone stairways around trees and creeks, allowing nature to decorate as she chose.

From my window, I could see the vast maze and into the forest beyond. I could even see the center of the maze and... I paused mid-bite. Lady Venom was bathing in a pond in the center of the maze. I wondered how many victims had died before making it to that pond with its crystal blue water. She dunked under and emerged, running her fingers over her wet hair and standing, exposing her full breasts and hard pink nipples. Flushing, I tried to pull away, knowing it was improper—and downright creepy—to watch someone in such a private state. But I couldn't peel my gaze from her form, her curves, her skin. Every piece of her was more breathtaking than the last. Steam rose from her head and shoulders in the cool spring air, making her appear as a smoking mythical being.

And then, as if she'd been aware of my stare the entire time, she glanced up, making intentional eye contact, the crystal shade of her irises piercing through me like the daggers in the necks of her victims from the prior day. I wasn't entirely sure she wouldn't rain the same fate down upon me for improperly gawking.

Embarrassed and breathless, I shut the curtains and hastily changed out of my nightgown. The armoire was filled with clothing, but that wasn't what surprised me. What surprised me was the presence of both dresses and slacks. As if to say I could wear pants if I wanted. I'd only ever worn pants as a child, and only gowns as a lady of bidding age. The pair of brown trousers I stepped into fit me perfectly and hugged my hips in a way that said they certainly were not made for men. As I buttoned them and slipped on a fitted silk blouse, I surveyed myself in the mirror. For once, I was pleased with what a saw. I was still a few shades too pale and dusted with light auburn freckles to match my unruly curls. But it was better than a white goose wedding dress. I sent a silent thank you to Lady Venom and her ghosts for allowing me such a small but meaningful freedom as being able to choose my own clothing.

Peeking into the hallway, I saw no rats or skeletons or, scarier, *snakes.* So I tiptoed down the corridor and descended the spiral staircase. My hand slid down the railing and bumped against something cold. Suddenly, I realized it was a long, thick, black snake.

I sprang backward and screamed, jumping in place, as if to shake off the nerves or the feeling of its scales on my skin. The snake only glided down the railing, flicking its tongue as it went. Scurrying past it, I eased open the front door and ran down the stairs. I wasn't entirely sure where I was going or what I was doing when the sound of a puff of air and stomp against gravel pulled my attention.

Darting around the maze, ignoring every colorful branch in my path, I found the source of the noise beneath a willow tree, and my heart rejoiced at the sight of my horse, Penny. She bowed her head as Lady Venom stroked her blond mane. I approached carefully, not sure if she'd yell at me or slit my throat for watching her bathe earlier.

But instead of meeting me with contempt, she flicked me a fleeting glance before saying, "Trousers suit you. And that shade of emerald is lovely on you as well."

"Thank you for the room. And the clothes and food. And you know, for saving my life yesterday." I fiddled with a stray thread on my pants, knowing I sounded like an idiot. "You're also beautiful," I added on at the end too quickly. I was nowhere near as smooth and charming as she was.

Her eyes skimmed over me again. "There's no need to be afraid of me. I don't bite."

"Yes, but do you poison and torment men?"

"I don't bite."

The giggle that erupted from my chest was doubly improper, and I heard my mother's faint voice in my head, scolding me for finding such a thing funny. But when I met the lady's gaze, she was only smiling softly.

"You're kind to animals but murder humans?" I asked, sincerely curious as I watched her soft caress of Penny, knowing that only hours earlier, those same hands had wielded knives.

"Not humans. *Men*," she replied, pulling a carrot from her bag and feeding it to the grateful mare. "And animals are better than both, regardless. Your horse is very kind. She will be loyal to you for a long time."

"Technically, she's not mine," I replied, petting Penny's middle. "She's my husband's."

Lady Venom stepped closer, leaning on the side of the large beast, almost daring me to stumble backward with her proximity. But I steeled my stance and focused on the feel of fur and not the otherworldly scent of orchids and spice from Venom's shining dark hair.

"You aren't married," she said plainly.

I cleared my throat. "Well, no. Not technically. I, um, ran away from my wedding yesterday. The man who won me at the bidding was"—I shook my head—"too terrible to fathom. I thought I'd risk it all by coming into your woods, never thinking for a moment I'd actually happen upon you, let alone live to tell the tale."

"Well, I'm still deciding whether you'll live or die." She said it so simply I glanced up to find another soft smile. I let out a giggle of relief at her joke. At least, I hoped she was joking. Lady Venom wore another form-fitting, slinky gown. Only this one was a deep shade of burgundy. She was a dark queen of lore, and it took effort not to stare in infatuation.

"I'm sorry about earlier. I didn't know about the bathing pool and—"

"Did you like what you saw?"

Heat flooded my face and dropped to my core in the same instant. What was I supposed to say? *You're the most beautiful creature I've ever seen? I could get lost in your curves for all of eternity and it wouldn't be enough?* Then I remembered her baiting and flirting with the men from yesterday before she killed them and wondered if this was some sort of test on whether I should live or die. There was so much to decipher with her, and I didn't know which part in her game I played.

So I only looked at my shoes. "Again, I'm really sorry, ma'am."

When I glanced back up, I couldn't help but notice her face fall ever so slightly. *No, no, no. Why did I say that? Did she want one of my truer answers?*

Pushing off the horse, she turned to leave. "This is your home now, Poesy," she said over her shoulder. "Get comfortable, explore, find something that brings you enjoyment. Oh, and meet me for dinner each evening in the dining room."

I swallowed. "I'm not staying here forever." I couldn't possibly reside in this house of horrors, tripping over my words as often as I did with the snakes. This place was dangerous for so many reasons. My growing attraction to its lady being the biggest and most lethal.

"Oh, but you are. And trust me when I say there is no escaping me. You'll grow to like it, and perhaps even to tolerate me." With that, she departed as gracefully as a dove on a soft wind. I wanted to do so much more than tolerate her, and I had the distinct impression I'd hurt her feelings. Why did that bother me as deeply as it did? And why wasn't I as terrified as I should have been?

Instead, her words about keeping me captive only excited and warmed something within me, and I couldn't help but fantasize about what that might entail. Captured by the beast in the woods. The serpent queen.

CHAPTER SIX

Upon Edith's insistence, I'd dressed for dinner. I'd chosen another emerald green shade. It was soft and flowy and not at all uncomfortable like the bidding dresses. Hope fluttered in my heart that maybe Lady Venom would like it. That maybe she'd find me as beautiful as I found her.

A melody on a piano drew me toward the dining room. Still, the untamed beauty of the manor was brilliant. Vines twisting over every iron chandelier. The walls perfectly cluttered with paintings, pasted on letters, even kiss prints. One of the cursive scrawled letters was signed with a dark scarlet kiss print with, *Love, Red*, signed in big swirly font. It looked like a home someone had lived in for a very long time, and that made me curious about whether the striking and mysterious woman playing the piano was as young as her face portrayed.

Lady Venom's icy blue stare hooked me from above the instrument as she stood and glided over. The candlelight deepened her features to hues as rich as the berry and jewel shades it seemed she preferred to surround herself with. "Thank you for joining me. You look lovely." She took my hands, and I flushed at the innocent contact. "Though you aren't required to wear gowns or act like a bell of the ball, as the ghosts are calling you. Please, dress however you like."

"You've been very generous," I replied, unable to think of much other than how her dark blue silk dress dipped down her cleavage enough to make my mouth water. How soft and supple her breasts looked… Suddenly I wasn't hungry for dinner, but for her. Only for her.

"Not too terrible for a captor, I suppose." She smirked, pulling out my chair and ushering me to sit. "I do hope you enjoy the meal. If not, let me know what you like, and I'll inform the cooks to prepare it for you."

I took in the sight that was more opulent than I could have ever imagined. And for being a woman so fierce, Lady Venom had been incredibly kind so far. Somehow, the woman filling my wineglass was the same eliciting screams from the woods, screams that made her the topic of scary stories in my town.

After she took a seat across from me, I downed my greens and potatoes before forking the meat. "Is this… is this bodies of the men you've killed?"

Venom raised her dark brows before placing a delicate hand to her chest and letting out a melodic laugh that sprang a smile to my own face. To see her laugh, to be the cause of that laughter…

"Men would taste disgusting." She took a sip of her wine, still chuckling. "Could you imagine? No, bellflower. That is duck. However, I wouldn't mind a taste of you."

Almost choking on my buttery bite, I washed it down with the fruit forward red beverage. Was this all a ploy to fatten me up and… eat me? And why did that idea send jolts of lightning to the spot between my thighs?

But before I could entertain a response better than the one I'd offered earlier, I yelped, almost spilling my drink. A striped red and yellow snake was slithering down the table runner. "Why so many snakes?" I whined, inching back in my seat. "They're so terrifying. Truly, I hate them." My breathing quickened as I spotted more that I hadn't noticed as one slid down the piano keys, bringing about a brash and eerie sound.

Lady Venom stroked a gentle finger over the striped serpent as it made its way down the table's leg. "Yes. Such a shame you didn't wander into Lady Bunny's den. Alas, here we are. The snakes are extensions of me, in a sense. They feed off my mood. So they won't harm you. Unless you make me mad, that is."

"Oh, devils. I'm sure I'll eventually make you mad. Will you tell them not to bite me at least?" I begged. Though, despite my fear, my smile hadn't faded.

"Mm, but what about me? What if I want to bite you? It's me or the snakes." She swirled her wine seductively and pushed her chair out but didn't stand. "Come here, Poesy."

My body froze and ignited at the sound of her command. "You said you *don't* bite," I murmured weakly. Praying I could still remember how to stand, how to walk, I did as I was told. When I was within reach, she took my hands again and stood me in front of her as she sat like a queen on the throne. She gave my body a slow appraisal, her gaze sweeping to my feet and then ascending, pausing around my middle, my breasts, and resting on my eyes. My heart pounded in my chest as I awaited her every word and graceful movement.

"Do you know what it means to be a mistress?" she asked, her voice huskier than before.

I swallowed, suddenly feeling warm and tingly all over, fighting the urge to lean into her. "No," I admitted.

She stood then but pulled my palms toward her so my breasts collided with hers and our noses touched. Her breath was sweet as she spoke to the torrent of want raging inside me. "It means you will do, and be, anything I require. It means that I own you, your body. Your every desire and pleasure are mine."

"Yes," I whispered breathlessly.

"Good girl," she answered before lightly skimming my lips with hers. "Take this off," she ordered, spinning me around and unzipping the back of my dress.

The cool air hit my naked body as she eased my dress over my curves. With a swipe of her arm, silver trays and dishes crashed from the table to the floor, and before I could react, she grabbed my hips and brought me to face her again, only this time, a lithe hand pushed between my breasts and eased me onto the tabled behind me.

"What are we doing? What should I do?" I asked. I was nervous but also fully under her spell. Something deep within my soul wanted to please her, to make her happy.

Standing over me, she purred deep in her throat, peeling off my panties and assessing me as I lay back on the dining table. "I'll tell you exactly what to do, my sweet bellflower, and you will obey. Understood?"

I nodded eagerly. "Is—is it going to hurt?" I asked, not because I didn't want whatever she had planned, but more to prepare myself for the oncoming feeling. My mother had warned me that sex was painful. Lord Harkness had driven that point home as well with his threats. I was sure it would be unpleasant at first, but maybe, with her, I could come to like it.

Lady Venom took hold of my knees and spread them wide, coming to stand close to my aching center. "Yes, darling, this will hurt. This will be the most exquisite pain you've ever experienced. It will lead you down a path of many deaths by my hand and by your own. And you will crave every moment of my torment. Now, lie back. It is time for my dessert."

I did as commanded, lying back on shaking elbows. My legs trembled at her soft caress of my hips. Knowing her stare was on my most private of places sent thrills of heat and awareness through me. "You see," she coaxed so close to my pussy I could feel her warm breath. "I don't eat men, but women." She hummed in her throat. "You, I will devour." My hips writhed in response, and my breath came in short bursts of desire and intrigue. How could I want pain and hurt so desperately? I didn't know, but I was eager to find out. To learn anything she wanted to teach. To become Lady Venom's mistress. Leaning up on my elbows, I witnessed her look of desire as she sat at the head of the table, ready to sample me however she liked.

But when her eyes met mine, she reprimanded me gently. "Head on the table, my impatient flower. This time will be for feeling, not for watching."

This time. This time meant there would be more to come, and the thought sent butterflies raging through my ribs.

When my head pressed against the hard wooden table, the loss of control hit me. What would she do? And then her touch skimmed my inner thighs before brushing past my sex and landing to grip my ass. When her breath hit my core again, I whimpered out a question—one that had been rattling in my mind, but her touch set free. "What's your name? Your real name?"

She paused, and I wished I could see her face. After a long moment, she stood and leaned over me, her hips pressing again the wetness pooled around my center and making me suck in a warm lungful of air. Her attention went from my eyes to my breasts, and like she couldn't resist, she lightly caressed down my left tit before softly rolling my nipple between her thumb and forefinger.

My lips parted, and when my eyes drifted closed in pleasure from just her touch, she answered. "Alabaster Baudelaire."

There was no time to process the mysterious and lyrical name she'd given so freely. And then, somehow, she was more than Lady Venom. She returned to her seat, and I heard the screech of it moving closer. And this time, when I felt her breath, she didn't pause or hesitate. The tongue of my serpent queen flicked out and circled between my ass cheeks before gliding up my wet center. My hips instinctually thrust closer, wanting more, when her hands winged by her face, easing her thumbs along my slit and widening me for her tasting. When her tongue pushed into my opening, I whimpered, daring to reach my hands down and touch her hair. When she didn't flinch, instead sighing against me, I tangled her silky soft locks around my knuckles. "God, you're immaculate," I groaned. "I know I'm breaking the rules by watching. Don't make me lay my head back, please," I begged.

She opened her eyes and paused her ecstatic assault. Her raven black hair, dark purple flashes of hue, draped over my open hips, looking like a curtain in the snow. Somehow, as her eyes held mine while her perfect red lips dipped to my center, she wasn't Lady Venom. Yet she was more Lady Venom than ever before. I saw how both existed alongside Alabaster Baudelaire. The mysterious woman of horrors, of pain... of unimaginable pleasure.

"You may watch, but only because you asked so nicely. Though I hope you aren't frightened by what you see." She smirked, and my head spun with possibilities. "Oh, how I've wondered after your taste, darling foxglove..." She extended a slitted tongue, and I gasped the answer to my unspoken question, not able to process what I was seeing with what was happening. My legs trembled, and a squeak escaped my throat as her clipped tongue pinched my clit as precisely as any fingers could. "Ahh." She smiled and let out a seductive chuckle. "My little bellflower, what is this delightful flavor?"

My hands shivered into the waves of her hair, feeling each strand like velvet against my skin. "I want all of you," I whispered, breathless.

"You'll have me," she murmured, her soft breath grazing the air between my wet thighs. "But first I'll have you."

With the next glide of her soft finger down my slit, my head tilted back, and the world went hazy. She hummed in her alluring singsong chime. "No, none of that. You wanted to watch, so watch. I want your eyes on me while I consume every drop from your enchanting pussy."

When my gaze obediently met hers, she smirked and dropped her long black tongue playfully over her chin, allowing me to admire the triangle slit.

"You look purely and perfectly evil, right now," I said, awed. "My serpent queen."

"The venomous monster who's stolen her maiden. Yes, add it to my lore, please."

I giggled as her hands scooped under my ass cheeks again and gripped. Lowering once more, she inhaled. My face flushed at the feel of her nose pressed against my center. Her tongue flicked out again, meeting the path her fingers had just taken, and I moaned at the exquisite feel.

"Poesy, my dear. You taste..." She licked me from bottom to top, swirling around my clit with the movement and precision of one of her snakes, and I groaned. "You taste like hibiscus flowers and wild strawberries. Like my own personal temptress."

My fingers wove through her hair, twirling the locks around my wrists and letting stray strands fall. How long had her hair tempted me? How long had I dreamt of having it in my palms? It had been a day, but it felt like ages of want. My whole life puddled in desire for her, and I hadn't even known it.

"I don't think it's me doing the tempting here," I breathed. I was mesmerized by her, entranced by the way the light hit her lily skin, by every curve of her breasts, her hips, and her ass that came into view when she dipped lower, pushing her tongue deeper in its exploration.

While one hand held my ass firmly, the other slowly pushed up the center of me and ever so decadently inched two crossed fingers into my opening and a pinky finger in my ass. I pushed my hips forward, desperate for more, when her stare caught mine.

Not moving, she simply purred atop my cunt. "You are going to be my glorious, rapturous downfall, Poesy Laroche." Then she thrust her fingers in deeper, hooking them as she did. All while that terrifying tongue pinched and twirled my clit. The sensations were too much to bear. This must be the hurt she referenced. The most wonderful agony. Pleasure so intense it had nowhere else to go but pain. I never wanted it to end. I wanted to halt the conclusion that was building, but I was powerless in my chase for it all at once.

"That's it. Accept my first murder of you, Poesy. Give in. Swallow me whole," she purred, lips drenched and buzzing against me.

I screamed out, my hold tight on her, pulling at her hair and bucking in movements I'd never once made before now. This feeling was more than anything that I knew existed, and it exploded and shocked around me like death, like life, like beautiful bright colors and wine and every small smirk she'd blessed me with.

After wave upon wave riddled me speechless, her tongue kept lapping up my release, and her fingers kept tracing my walls, as if she were memorizing every piece of me inside and out. Another release built and erupted, and she sighed along with my moans, like my pleasure was the glass she drank from. That night, I supposed I was. My queen and I. Lady Venom the terrible. Alabaster Baudelaire the beautiful. And I was more her captive now than I ever thought possible. And now I no longer wanted to be free from her delicious prison.

CHAPTER SEVEN

The week was spent darker and more lavishly than I could have ever imagined in my small world of chickens and biddings and busybody mothers. I slept in, with no one to wake me. I ate all I wanted and sampled the most delicious foods I'd ever tasted. And after my first encounter with being a mistress for Lady Venom, the world seemed brighter, even amidst the snakes and skull planters. Though I shivered imagining whom the skulls formerly belonged to.

But I hadn't seen much of my lady since the night she made a meal of me on the dining room table. To my dismay, she hadn't been present at dinner since. Instead of sitting alone, I got braver in my explorations of my haunted house. The *branches* were getting easier to ignore as they mainly ignored me, too.

On this night, I couldn't sleep, and I was antsy about not having seen my lady in days. So I slipped on my dressing gown and grabbed a candle to light my way as I roamed the halls, praying I didn't trip over a *colorful branch*. Padding through the dining room, I stopped at the sound of voices in the kitchen. I made my way inside, expecting to see several people, but it was empty. Odd... but my stomach growled despite my hearty beef stew dinner, so I rummaged around. I was pulling a baguette and a block of cheese from a cabinet when the murmurs reignited behind me. When I looked, it was nothing again. That was, until something shimmered in the moonlight. I would have missed it if I hadn't kept staring. "Is someone there?" I asked. "Edith, Paul?"

The shimmer materialized into a translucent form. No, *four* forms materialized around me. I swallowed, rubbing my neck, realizing they'd been here watching me this whole time. How much had they seen of the past few days? I blushed, remembering my blissful encounter in the dining room.

"Hello, I'm Meg. And this is Arthur, Clara, and Timothy." She smiled, and the see-through people stared back at me as I clutched a baguette and a block of cheese like some renegade rat.

"It's nice to meet you all. Are there... more ghosts coming?"

The ladies giggled. "We've been here the whole time," she replied, floating through the table and straight for me. "But we only appear when we trust someone." Meg reached behind me and pulled down a plate, taking my baguette and cheese and proceeding to slice it up for me.

"Thank you," I said gratefully. "So, do you guys like working here?" I struggled to find the right questions to ask. They were *ghosts*, after all. What was appropriate to say to the dead?

"Love it," Timothy answered, flying over and putting on a teakettle. "Lady Venom is most gracious to allow us to stay and haunt in plain sight."

Another girl ghost giggled. "Plus, it is such fun scaring the stupid men who try to come here."

"The ones who make it past the snakes and plants, and Venom herself, that is," Arthur added, tipping his hat at me before floating out the door.

I accepted the plate from Meg and leaned against the counter, nibbling the cheese and watching them work. They were much nicer than Edith, so I felt compelled to stay and get to know them. And also dig for a little more information on my captor. "So, um, how did Lady Venom come to be here and employ you all?"

The teakettle whistled, and Timothy poured several mugs of the hot, minty concoction. "That's a story best heard from our lady herself," he said after a moment, handing me the tea.

"So you're the new mistress," Meg said in awe, resting her chin on her knuckles and watching me drink. She didn't look much older than me, and it was hard to tell in the dim light, but she looked to have wavy reddish brown hair tied back in a lavender ribbon.

Fear and suspicion mixed with jealousy trickled down my spine. "Have there been many mistresses?"

Timothy cleared his throat as Meg opened her mouth to speak, causing her to shut it and give me a sympathetic gaze. "She'll tell you what she wants you to know. Trust her," Meg assured, giving my shoulder a squeeze.

The remaining ghosts flitted past, off to do... whatever ghosts did, and I called out to Meg as she reached the doorway. "Any advice on how to get her to trust me?"

The lovely spirit paused in contemplation before smiling. "She loves cherries. Try that."

And with that, she walked through the closed door, leaving me truly alone in the kitchen this time. The legend and mystery of my lady deepened with each passing day, and so did my curiosities about who she was, about what she was. But Alabaster was a woman who, I had a feeling, would be a puzzle worth solving. And I was up for the challenge.

CHAPTER EIGHT

I woke the next morning with an ache between my thighs. She'd licked me so deliciously that, despite my nightly bath, I'd been wetter for her with every passing day. That morning, I couldn't keep it at bay no longer. The sun dusted in, and I stretched beneath my sheets, my skin feeling tender and hyperaware as it rubbed against my silk nightgown.

How could I replicate the feel of her mouth against my center? Was anything in existence as soft and inviting as her supple lips? My mind floated in a half-asleep haze, picturing her full breasts as she leaned over me. I wondered what she tasted like and if she'd ever let me do to her what she'd done to me. My mouth watered at the thought, and the ache grew between my inner thighs. Kicking off my already damp panties, along with the sheet, I lay exposed for a moment, letting the cool air taunt my bare waist and contemplating the lengths my morning desire would push me, too.

In delirium, I grabbed my plush pillow and rose onto my knees. My brain didn't have the time to talk me out of it. Instead, I shoved it between my thighs. The pillowcase was cool, and ridges formed in just the right places. Slowly, I bucked my hips against the fabric, closing my eyes and pretending it was her instead. Imagining her lying beneath me, letting me rub against her in any way I pleased.

The friction coaxed me further, and I reached between myself and the pillow, opening my eyes to reposition, but startled.

There she was. Lady Venom leaned against my bedpost, arms crossed and head cocked, taking in the sight. "How—how long have you been—" I stammered out, making to move, but she held up a palm to halt me.

"No, please don't stop on my account. Continue."

My face flushed with embarrassment but also with desire. Maybe she wanted to watch me like this. Maybe it brought her some form of pleasure or happiness. What made her happy? I desperately wanted to know and become whatever it was. I swallowed. "Okay."

She sat on the edge of the bed and extended her hand. I sighed in surprise when she eased it between my sex and the pillow, her deft fingers slicking down my center and swirling around my clit. "Here. Now your clit has something to ride against. And just like this, I'll spread your pussy lips." She tugged the pillowcase up before removing her hand.

"I want your hand though," I whimpered when she placed it back in her lap.

But she only shook her head. "And I want to watch what you were doing when you thought I wasn't looking. Go on, hump your pillow for me, bellflower."

Letting out a sound that was a mixture of a whine and a pant, I did as she instructed, my core and the pillow perfectly positioned now. "I was imagining that this was you beneath me," I dared to whimper as my hips began to move. Each stroke was more animated this time, skimming along my slit just right. And with my lady's crystal eyes on me, her cleavage so sinfully demure, those perfect, black painted lips...

"Were you now?" she teased. "And were you thinking of these?" She ran a palm over her breasts. "Or this?"

I gawked, breathlessly still moving my hips as I watched her opposite hand slip between her thighs. She was still in her nightgown, too. It was thin and silky, and I could make out her erect nipples and the wetness that expanded on the fabric as she touched it to her pussy. "Both," I admitted. "All of you."

"Would you like to watch me come?" Lady Venom asked, resting her head against the bedpost. "Because I'd like to come with you."

"Oh my god, yes," I replied, breathless, my release building to an excruciating level. "Please."

"Such a good mistress," she praised, tugging up her skirts, pulling them up around her hips. Her hand slipped into the exposed space, and I avariciously watched, almost forgetting the pillow, the bed, the world, even existed. Two fingers slipped into her opening, then reemerged to circle her clit. She was so elegant and poised, her breathing heavy as her fingers worked. Our perfume of combined passion made the air heavy with impending delight. "I can't hold out any longer," I cried. "Please come with me," I begged.

Her delicate groan and the rosy flush across her lily pale cheeks were my undoing. Flashes of elation sparked across my vision as we ebbed and flowed, watching the other's pleasure. When my knees were weak from the exertion and bliss, I climbed off and pulled down my gown to sit next to her.

But no sooner had I, than she took my hand. "Come, I'll draw you a bath."

"Will you join me?" I asked, so full of hope she chuckled softly.

"Perhaps."

I'd take a perhaps over a no any day.

After she turned a knob, the tub filled with steaming hot water. "This place runs on magic," I said, awed, as the aroma of jasmine danced in the morning air.

"I'm glad you think so," Lady Venom purred, coming up behind me and tugging my gown. "Lift your arms."

After she undressed me, she offered me a hand and helped me into the tub. "Join me?" I practically begged, eliciting a small giggle that echoed off the marble tile.

"Scoot forward, and don't turn around," she ordered. And before I could argue or ask her meaning, she stepped in behind me, thrilling me with her closeness as her legs wrapped around me from behind. "Now lean back. Let me wash you."

She was so demanding, but in a self-assured way that left me not only eager to please her, but dying to. What she ordered was what I wanted. It sounded like commands, but truly, it was her reading my mind before I'd thought of it. Could it stay like this? Could I just be empty and ordered about by my lady forever?

The only sounds were water trickling as her delicate hand lathered a rough, round sponge and moved it down my arms. "Where have you been the past few days?" I asked.

"Places to go, men to kill," she murmured. I wholly could not conclude whether it was serious or a joke, so I changed the subject.

"Where do the ghosts come from?"

"Near and far. I see you've met more of them now. Beware that Arthur is a horrible gossip, though his lemon cake is divine."

I giggled, feeling Lady Venom's nose press into my hair as she inhaled, breathing me in. She whispered in my ear. "I do adore the sound of your laugh, bellflower."

Maybe I should have soaked in her waters of kindness and allure without a second thought, but there was still so much I wanted to know about her and this brand-new world that slithered and floated by me. "How many mistresses have you had?"

She moved the sponge over my breasts, the rough and wet scratch of it raising my nipples and causing them to ache after her. My want for her was insatiable, and I wished she'd let me turn around and get a look at the soft, naked, wet body I leaned against.

Humming a gentle melody, she finally replied. "Forty-seven."

"Oh," I sighed, feeling a flurry of conflicting feelings swell within me. "What were they like?"

"Some despised me. A few tolerated me. None have responded as well or as quickly as you." Her teeth tugged at my earlobe, squeezing a sigh from my throat. "You're so special. Aren't you?"

"What happened to them?" I breathed, afraid to hear the answer.

Her hand slipped the sponge between my thighs and pressed against my center. "They weren't you."

An odd answer, but my mind and body were now wholly focused on her touch and the feel of her warm, soft thighs around my waist. She twined her legs with mine, forcing them to open as she moved the sponge. It didn't take long before I was panting and writhing as she held me. Then, suddenly, she let go of the sponge and replaced it with her fingers.

"That's it. Give me more," she hummed against my neck, letting her sharp incisors pinch at my skin. It reminded me of her devilish snake tongue and the way she looked at me as she tasted the places her fingers now explored. Another shock of bliss shuddered through me. I arched my back and moaned into the echoes of the room, hoping the sound of my song could scare away the lingering memories of mistresses past as they haunted me now more than the real ghosts of the manor.

CHAPTER NINE

Lady Venom departed from my bath and my touch, disappearing like the enigma she was. Leaving me sore and sated but dying for more. To have her in my bed, to look at her naked body and touch her as I liked. The thought gnawed at me. Why'd she leave? Where did she go?

If she trusted me more, if I was indeed a better mistress than the others before me, maybe she'd tell me. Maybe someday she'd take me with her. I wondered how long I had here. As much as I melted into the idea of being hers forever, of exploring her mind and mystique for all of time, I knew my days were numbered. Lord Harkness wouldn't soon forget the embarrassment of being left at the altar. His men would come back, maybe in greater numbers than before. What kind of coward was I, staying put and inviting hell upon my lady and her home? Shame tensed my shoulders, and I grabbed a basket from the kitchen. I'd chatted with Meg as she went about her chores. Today, she was cleaning dust off the leaves of the plants that dangled from the ceiling. Floating had its perks, I supposed.

A snake dropped in front of her polishing, and she yelped. "Sneaky little things." She giggled, giving the black snake a pet before continuing. "Where are you off to this afternoon?"

Looking up at her where she was flitting around the chandelier, I held out my basket. "Cherry picking."

"Oh, you've got it bad."

"Got what bad?"

"Nothing," she replied in a singsong voice. "It's adorable."

When I leaned against the cold banister of the spiral staircase, something shifted, like the post was loose. I inspected it closer, and it clicked out of the way, revealing a compartment and an item beneath. Picking it up, I twirled it in my grip.

"Oh," Meg commented. "Looks like you found one of the lady's knives."

"She has knives in the staircase?" I asked, liking the weight of it in my hand.

Meg giggled, moving on to a new vine. "She has knives everywhere. I'm surprised this is the first you've found." The ghost's gaze whispered over me, and something like hesitation passed over her face before she went back to her task. "Take it with you. Lady Venom won't mind. It may help you cut through the stubborn, stuck cherries."

Tossing it into my basket, I thanked her and made my way outside. Down the mossy cobblestone steps, past the large purple blooms that turned their petals to watch after me as I walked by. The ghosts in the kitchen assured me the fruit trees were near the manor, and I spied them in the distance where they said they'd be. But murmurs behind the maze caught my attention and stilled my pace. My mother would have scolded me for crouching behind a thicket to listen, but something told me this was the quickest way to learn any of the secrets of this place. Because Lady Venom and the ghosts didn't seem keen to give me much more than tiny riddles in response to my questions.

"She's up to at least five men killed. This isn't good," one voice said. Peering through the leaves, I spotted what looked to be Edith. She floated back and forth with her arms crossed.

A man's voice sighed. "This mistress could be the one. Have faith, darling." Paul, I realized, though my chest constricted at his words.

Edith huffed. "You have to be joking. Look at her. She's clueless, witless, and a lost mouse in a den of vipers. No, Poesy surely does not have what it takes, and we are dangerously close to seven before—"

"We make it to seven every year and never pass it. We must trust our lady," Paul assured.

Something cool moved over my hand, and I suppressed a scream at the sight of a bright green snake wrapping around my wrist.

"No, no, get off," I whisper-whined, inching away from the thicket. Grabbing my basket, I took off in a slow run. "What was that about? Why does my presence here matter, and how does the number of men killed play into anything at all?" I asked myself as I caught my breath under a canopy of cherry trees. They smelled like Lady Venom, and the thought of her warmed my lower belly. Something tightened around my wrist, and I looked down to realize the small terror had accompanied me. "Get off," I pleaded, shaking my hand gently next to a tree branch. "Go on, slither off to find your buddies."

Its pink tongue flicked out, tickling against my skin as it rested its leafy green head on its scaled body.

"Ugh." I sighed. "You're a tiny bit cute for something so terrifying," I admitted. "Let's pick some cherries, and then maybe Meg will know how to unlatch you. Don't bite me, okay?"

I gathered the ripest looking fruits I could find, admiring their deep red shades and only slightly ignoring the slitted eyes and flicker of tongues I came across beneath the leaves. God, there were serpents everywhere here. But surprisingly, they never tried to harm me. They just watched curiously and then went about their snake business. And somehow, oddly, it felt nice not being alone. Like maybe they'd accepted me as a friend now. Sort of like the new ghosts who revealed themselves every day. I'd met over a dozen of them now, and each time an apparition began to glimmer into solidity, pride swelled in my heart that something about me gained an invisible force's trust. Maybe it was the same with the snakes, though I had no idea what I'd done to convey my trustworthiness.

And I had even less of an idea of what I'd just overheard Edith and Paul discussing. My mother would say this is why it's rude to eavesdrop. But is it still rude if the subject of the conversation is you? I popped a ripe cherry into my mouth once my basket was full, ignoring my new bracelet, and turned my back to the trees to make my way back to the manor. But suddenly, something rough latched on to my mouth. One of the lord's men had discovered me and proceeded to drag me backward. And now I was going to be taken back to my guillotine.

CHAPTER TEN

A scream strangled in my throat as I held on to the arm of a man, my basket's handle falling into the crook of my elbow. "Quiet, or I'll make it hurt," the man hushed roughly, dragging me beyond the fruit trees and into the forest. My kicks and fighting were nothing compared to how big he was. Then I remembered the knife. If I could only reach it. "Stop fighting it, you little whore. What have you done to not be killed by the lady of the woods, huh?" he mocked as my heels scraped against branches. "Son of a bitch!" he cried, releasing his grip on my head. I fell to the ground and turned back in time to see my bracelet snake move from the man's bleeding hand to strike his jaw.

It gave me just enough time to pour out my cherry basket and grab the knife. I held it up with a shaky hand as the man shook off the green snake and held his red and marred jaw. He chuckled darkly as he stepped forward. "Those green ones aren't poisonous," he growled. "But that hurt, so now I'll make you hurt, too. And oh, we both know your husband is ready to punish you real good for that stunt you pulled. Best come with me—"

He paused as the knife trembled in my palm. I took a step back. The man looked over my shoulder and raised a wary eyebrow. "You must be her. You don't look so poisonous to me. I bet my lord would take delight in breaking you just like he plans to break her."

Glancing over my shoulder, I saw my savior. She stood in a long lapis velvet dress with her arms crossed, as if she were merely disappointed with the intruder. She clicked her tongue and strode forward, her long trumpet sleeves floating behind her. "Venom," she corrected.

The man took out his own knife then. He'd mocked her, but the closer she got, the greater the fear flashed in his eyes. "W-what?" he stammered, holding a much larger knife than mine. "Don't come any closer."

My lady gave me an almost imperceptible coy flash of incisor before looking back at Lord Harkness's man. "The snake that bit you isn't *poisonous* because no snake is. Snakes are *venomous*. Venom is *injected*, not *ingested* like poison. My plants, they are poisonous." She mused, kneeling to pick up a cherry from my basket. As she plopped the fruit into her mouth, the cowardly man took the opportunity to lunge for her. I screamed in warning, but I was too late.

Lady Venom stood and turned, the man falling onto his front. Before he could turn over, she placed a boot on his back and pushed him back down. "I considered sending you back with a warning to your men. But now you've gone and pissed me off."

"Please," he begged. "Please just let me go, miss."

"Venom," she purred again. "That's Lady Venom to you. And I'm afraid your lesson on the matter isn't over." She moved the sharp heel of her leather boot to the man's thick neck. He squirmed against her but wisely, or foolishly, stopped fighting with brawn and began to beg.

But it didn't matter. Her smirk met my gaze, and with a swift kick, her heel cut into his throat. The man yelled out, and I covered my mouth with my hands, not entirely sure what I was witnessing. And then he started to shake, violently writhing and groaning. His body constricted, and when he rolled over, foam was bubbling from his lips and down his bloodied scruff.

Lady Venom breezed past him and knelt by my basket, scooping the cherries back in as the man tremored out a slow and agonizing death.

"W-what's happening to him?" I whispered hoarsely, not realizing I was still pointing the knife in front of me.

She regarded the object and glided forward. "He's learning the difference between poison and venom. I lace all my things in venom." She shrugged. "For good measure. This particular strain is rattlesnake." She paused and smiled, reaching into the tree above me. "Ah, speak of the devil." When her hands reemerged, she held a thick, deadly-looking snake in her hands. I only trembled more eagerly at the sight. It wasn't the almost-cute little garden bracelet from before. This was a giant diamond-headed, slitted-eyed beast with jagged, pointed scales. It rattled the end of its tale like some demonic purr as she stroked it with the back of her finger.

Taking its head between her thumb and forefinger, she pressed, and it opened its mouth, revealing hooked teeth. As if the thing needed a way to look even more menacing than before. "Curious little things, rattlesnakes. You can hold them by the head, like this, but their fangs can rotate at a 180-degree angle." The serpent wiggled its fangs but didn't harm her. It was as if he was helping in her demonstration. "All it would take is one prick of the thumb, and their venom would shock through you. But, even more fascinating, are the properties contained within the venom itself. There's a specific element within it that induces fear. The little thing wants you to fear it." She returned the snake gently to his branch as I watched, in awe of my dark lady. "If you're afraid, your heart speeds up, pumping blood through your body, accelerating the venom's affect. Fear does that, doesn't it? Speeds along our demise, perpetuates venom." She crossed her arms and glanced over her shoulder. "This gentleman was very afraid, as you can see. He died in under a minute from the venom on my shoe. You..." She looked me up and down as I still stood frozen with the knife against my sweaty palm. "Are likewise afraid."

"Yes, I am always afraid," I admitted on a breath, something I'd scarcely allowed myself to even think.

Lady Venom hummed. "If *I* can see the knife, you're holding it wrong. If *you* can see the knife, you know that your attacker doesn't know how to use it. Like this dead fellow behind me. However..." In an instant, she moved around me with the grace of a swan. Her breasts pressed against my shoulder blades, and her hand covered mine, fingering the weapon and sliding the blunt side of the blade against my wrist and lowering my arm. "Hold it like this, hidden, and you'll actually have a fighting chance. And if you see someone else hiding their knife, chances are, they know how to use it, and you should run if you know what's good for you. Practice. You'll get it."

I swallowed, invigorated by the idea of practice. "Can I have more knives?" I asked, noticing she didn't move away, only held me there.

"You can have whatever you like," she whispered in my ear, chilling and warming me at once.

Leaning back into her touch, I ran my hands down her velvet-covered arms. "Okay, I'd like to make you something for dessert tonight. So stay out of the kitchen."

Her lithe giggle sent butterflies darting into my chest. "As you wish, mistress." She let me go, and when I turned, she was scooping something from the grass. "It seems you have a new friend." Holding up her wrist, the wide-eyed green snake balanced forward, as if seeking me out. "Some old witch stories would call him your familiar." Despite my previous terror, a smile curved my lips as I reached out my palm, allowing the creature to curl around my arm again.

"Well, he did bite a man for me, so I guess this one isn't so bad."

"I believe snakes are growing on you," Lady Venom chided, but she was smiling, and I swooned at the sight.

"Maybe. Maybe lots of things are growing on me," I replied, giving my scaly bracelet a pet.

Lady Venom backed away, waving her trumpet sleeves. "Enjoy the rest of your day, bellflower."

I suppressed the urge to run after her. "You will join me for dessert this evening, right?"

"Mmm, you know I love sweet things." She unfurled her forked tongue, making me gasp and clench my thighs at the obscene sight of it. And with that, she left me alone in the cherry grove. Only me, the snakes, the cherries, and the dead man being swallowed whole by a python.

CHAPTER ELEVEN

Despite the ease of trousers, I slipped on the fuchsia gown that Edith had laid out for me. My protests died on my lips when I recalled Lady Venom's innuendo of sweets... and remembered the last sweets between my thighs that she tasted on the dining room table. Oh, how I hoped for a repeat. But first, I had to arrive early to make my own treat for her.

"A man died to make this pie. It better be good," I joked to Meg, and her giggling paused.

"Really?" she asked, glancing at Timothy, who was brewing tea. Only the passing glances of worry were discernible in my see-through friends.

I wiped my hands on my apron as Timothy floated over and took the dish, placing it in the oven without a word. "He was trying to harm me," I defended my lady.

Meg sat on the edge of the counter. "It's not that. Any man that wanders close to this place deserves the death that comes for him. It's just that she can only kill so many before..." Meg looked over her shoulder at Timothy and gave me a pained expression, as if she wanted to say more but couldn't in mixed company. I nodded in understanding. "Anyway, I think she will love the pie."

"I hope so." I peeked out the door into the dining room, seeing that Lady Venom had not yet arrived.

Moments later, I sat at the dining room table with a steaming cherry pie, garnished with a fresh cherry on top, proudly smoothing my skirt and waiting for my lady to arrive. The ghosts brought a meal of steamed carrots and salmon before evaporating through the walls, leaving me alone with food and whatever snake companions were wrapping around the candlesticks. My garter snake slid off my wrist to join them, and I smiled, watching him play. What was happening to me?

Time ticked forward, and I poked absentmindedly at my roasted carrots, until Arthur came to clear the dishes. I stopped him. "Wait, isn't Lady Venom coming?"

He seemed to have rosy cheeks for a ghost, and I thought that a cute quality for a spirit to have. With a jolly smile, he answered. "If she isn't here by now, she's not coming."

"Do you know where she goes?"

Arthur cleared my plate and looked around, as if to check if anyone was listening, before leaning in and whispering, "Our lady's room is in the west wing."

I blinked, surmising that the information he shared was something he wasn't supposed to tell me. "Thank you," I answered, picking up the now cold pie. "Um... do you think someone could bring the little green snake to my room? I don't want him to wonder where I went."

Arthur tipped his hat. "Of course, Mistress Poesy."

Mistress Poesy was right, and Mistress Poesy wasn't about to be stood up. She said she'd come. Taking a sharp left, I stomped all the way to the west wing. The decor turned to dark shades until the wallpaper and furnishings were all black on this side of the manor. It had a more forbidden air than the rest of the house, and that was saying something, because this place was level-ten creepy at all times. But I'd gotten used to the pretty charm within the eerie. The ghosts were kind, the snakes were gentle, and the flowers mixed within the skulls were... endearing in a strange way. Black wax dripped onto wax mountains that lit the hall as I reached an ebony door with a snake skull handle. *How very like her,* I thought.

Hesitating, I worked up the courage to knock. No answer. I knocked again. Briefly, I considered leaving, but then I recalled how she'd just waltzed into my room when I'd been just waking up and having a private moment in bed. Well, now it was my turn to waltz, and I hoped she'd dance with me.

As I turned the knob, anticipation fluttered. The door swung open, unlocked. The space was vast, with high ceilings draped in black fabric and strung with black vines. Only a short candle on a desk flickered, indicating someone was here. Gripping the pie, I tiptoed in, feeling this was a mistake.

"Hello?" I murmured, thinking I would just turn and run. Maybe she hadn't heard me.

The door slammed behind me, startling a scream from my throat. When I turned around, I gasped, seeing Lady Venom cock her head and assess me. My brain couldn't compute what she was wearing... A black leather corset sat above thin silk panties, fishnet stockings, and heels.

"What a naughty mistress I have," she cooed, clicking a lock on the door. "How shall I punish you?"

Heat dropped to my pussy at her words. "You said you'd come and have the dessert I made you, and you didn't show—"

"Did I say I'd come?"

"Yes," I argued.

"I don't think I did," she taunted, circling me. It was then I noticed that she dragged something behind her, long and slender... and then I realized.

"A horse whip?" I questioned. "What is that for?"

"Bend over and find out," she quipped, giving the ground a snap that made me jump. "You look so innocent in pink, Poesy. So ready to be corrupted by me."

"You know what I think?" I dared, meeting her stare as she put her hands on her hips in front of me and arched a dark eyebrow. "I think you aren't as tough as you act. I think you're afraid."

"Me, afraid? Never," she scoffed lightly. "Put that on the desk." With a small huff, I walked backward, not taking my eyes off her, until my ass bumped into the desk. I sat the pie down. She chuckled. "What are you doing?"

"Not taking my eyes off you. I don't want to be hit with that thing."

"Oh, but you will. You'll beg for it before too long."

"I highly doubt that," I replied, but it came out on a breath that betrayed my interest.

With a gentle hand, she moved my hair and planted a soft kiss on my shoulder. "Palms on the desk," she whispered.

My breathing picked up. "What?"

"Do as I say."

I growled under my breath as I turned, cursing the damned pie as I looked at it, feeling air hit my backside as my skirt was pulled over my ass. Lady Venom then grabbed my underwear and yanked them down, leaving me bare. "Brace yourself, mistress," she cooed.

"I don't want to be hit," I said again, knowing there was nothing to do, no way to stop it. I'd disobeyed my lady.

"Shh," she coaxed. "And keep your hands right there."

Bracing myself for impact, I felt her cool hands rub my backside before her thumbs parted my cheeks. Before I could question it, a moan fled my mouth as her warm mouth encompassed my asshole. It was salacious and wicked. The sensation was indescribable in all its sinister delight, and I rested my elbows on the desk to give her more access. She groaned between my cheeks, flicking her forked tongue around my hole. Her saliva dripped onto my cunt, and her tongue soon followed, pushing into my opening while her hands spread me wide.

"Very good," she murmured against my center. "You are so wet for me, bellflower."

I moaned as her mouth found my clit and she sucked it hard while her fingers pushed into me. "This is wonderful punishment," I whimpered, feeling the combination of us drip down my inner thighs.

She hummed against my sensitive pussy. "You were kind enough to bring me dessert, though coming to my room uninvited is a crime in this manor."

"I didn't know that," I groaned against the desk as my cheek pressed against the cold wood. "But I'll be sure to break that rule again."

She giggled, the sound wet as she pumped in and out and licked my sex. "That's it, come on my mouth, Poesy."

It wasn't hard to obey a voice like that. My orgasm shuddered through me, making my knees buckle under my weight as stars danced behind my vision. I turned, leaning against the desk, finding

Lady Venom still on her knees, face glistening with me. "I want you like that," I confessed, breathless. Leaning forward, I dared tuck her hair behind her ears. "Let me?" I asked.

With a small smile, she stood and reached around me, pulling the pie off the table. "I'll let you feed me. How's that?"

"Not what I want..." I replied, my eyes roaming her body, noting how her pale breasts billowed atop the corset that hugged her voluptuous curves in all the right ways. "But I'd do anything you wanted me to."

Something that looked like a mix of sadness and compassion flitted across her delicate face. "Come, let's eat in bed."

So we did. I climbed into her high and enormous black bed, and she pulled two spoons from a bar cart. I scooped cherry pie into her mouth, and she did the same for me, laughing between bites at the decadence and absurdity of digging into a pie in bed.

A cool breeze wisped through the open window, and Lady Venom licked her spoon as she said, "I am aware that your upbringing and the disgusting ritual of bidding has bred fear in you. And I know that I am not what you hoped for when you wished for a partner in this life. Keeping you as my own has been... entirely selfish. Though, somehow, you have accepted this horrid fate with tremendous ease."

"Alabaster—" I interrupted, putting a hand on hers, but she lifted a palm to silence me.

"Want you I may, and as intense as I may be, I won't hurt you or harm you... well, without your desiring it, that is." Her crystal blue gaze fell to the fluffy comforter. "Please do accept my apologies if the whip scared you. I do enjoy my costumes."

A grin tugged at the corners of my mouth. "Yes, I've noticed."

The comfortable silence that stretched between us should have been filled with more from me. I should have told her that being captured by her had changed my life, but not in the way she thought. By taking my freedom, she'd given me more freedom than I'd ever had. And as far as a husband, I'd never desired a man or any person as much as I wanted her. Alabaster Baudelaire was slithering into my heart and soul, wrapping around my wrist and my ribs, and squeezing out anything that wasn't of her. And I welcomed my glorious death.

CHAPTER TWELVE

WHEN ALABASTER BAUDELAIRE TAKES your hand and pulls you through her poison garden, smiling like she has a secret she just can't wait to show you, you follow and try to keep your heart from bursting out of your chest. In truth, I'd follow her off a cliff and giggle the entire fall to the rocks below.

"Don't walk over this row of leafy babies. One touch of the Gympie-Gympie, and it would feel as if your body has been lit on fire and hit by lightning at the same time. Painful, though a fascinating way to watch men die." She sighed wistfully. "Keep your eyes closed,"

A giggle swept through me as she led me around the deadly Gympie and then allowed the petals of nicer flowers to brush my ankles as we walked hand in hand. "You blindfolded me, so that's not hard."

"You seem like a peeker," she goaded, eliciting more laughter.

She wasn't wrong. The chuckle of ghosts was heard as we passed, and I grinned like a fool, knowing we must have looked ridiculous. But I held on to the vision of my lady's beaming happiness as she'd tied the scarf around my eyes. When we stopped, she gripped my shoulders. "Okay, you can look now."

She tugged my blindfold, and I rubbed my chin, making sense of what I was looking at. "Scarecrows?" I asked, looking over my shoulder to see Lady Venom bouncing on her heels. It was so un-Lady Venom-like that it made me chuckle.

Paul floated over and dropped a big sack of flour, then faced us from under a cherry tree, where all the scarecrows stood propped against the trunk. And then Lady Venom handed me an ornate black box etched with snakes. "These are for you."

When I opened it, a breath left my lips and excitement rippled through my bones. "These are so beautiful," I breathed, running my fingers over six uniquely shaped ebony knives.

"They're yours. To practice, to keep, to kill," Lady Venom purred into my ear, warming me instantly. "I want you wearing them at all times."

"Will you teach me?" I asked, seeing that she held a knife of her own.

The corner of her mouth quirked, making her look catlike and dangerous. God, I loved that look. "I'm the only one allowed to teach you," she replied. "Now, let's start with throwing them and killing some scarecrows, shall we?"

I jumped in place, choosing a knife with the same purple hue as Alabaster's hair. "My mother never even let me touch the kitchen knives. I always thought handling them would be fun, but it wasn't suitable for a girl prepared for bidding." I weighed the heaviness of it in my palm, loving the potential it held. Could I be like Lady Venom? Could I kill as ruthlessly as she did if I had to? I wasn't sure of the answer, but knowing how to defend myself should Lord Harkness's men grab me again felt a lot like power, and power wasn't a sensation I was used to feeling. But Lady Venom brought about all sorts of new and wicked emotions inside me. Why not add deadly to the mix?

Alabaster spun her knife in her hand, and with a movement as graceful as a wolf, she sent the weapon swirling through the air until it went through a scarecrow's forehead, shaking the cherry tree behind it. Her skill awed me in a way that made me want to both kiss her and become her.

She hummed a tune, cupping my hand and repositioning my hold, then she stood behind me and guided my arm through the motions I'd just witnessed her take. It was like a dance, and she was teaching me the choreography. Though it took effort to focus on anything but her tart and sweet smell and the indescribable softness of her skin.

She whistled lightly before saying, "Goddess Diana was goddess of the hunt. I'd say she was still quite the lady, too. It's not either-or. We don't have to choose between strength and beauty. All women are inherently both. You are both a sweet bellflower and a deadly little foxglove."

Her words made me sigh and made my brain spin with possibilities of a life I'd scarcely allowed myself to imagine. A life without bidding ribbons and pushing out babies for men who didn't care for me. Oh, could I just live with her and our snakes and knives for all time? Being both soft and fierce with my Lady...

"Your list of names for me is growing," I teased as she let go of my arm, gesturing for me to try a throw.

So I did. Mimicking her, letting her seep into my blood, I let go of the knife. Curious snake eyes watched from their perches, squeezed against stones and hiding between flowers. And ghosts laughed, clapped, and pointed as my beautiful gift went charging into the grass with a thump. Lady Venom only handed me another. "We've got all day," she encouraged.

All day, all night, and forever, please?

CHAPTER THIRTEEN

THE WEEK CUT BY in a slash of flour in the wind and gutted hay from punctured scarecrows. The first time I finally hit one in the shoulder, I spun and laughed so hard even the ghosts were applauding. Lady Venom would stop by in the mornings and watch me from a balcony, holding a black parasol. Each day, a new dress and a new accessory, and I found myself looking forward to her getups. Though she hadn't said much more to me, and I was missing her wit along with her body.

But secretly, I loved to pretend I didn't know she was on a balcony watching me. Turning my back to her and feeling her stare sent tingles of electricity through me. I'd try to focus through the lovesick delirium and imagine that was what adrenaline would feel like. Lady Venom had explained that adrenaline was something snakes fed off. It was how they'd quicken the death of their prey, and half the battle of combat was keeping your emotions in check so you could think clearly.

Her standing above me, judging me like a dark goddess from her throne, sure worked in making my mind hazy. But even so, I was able to at least land my target more times than not. Meg had even stopped by a few times to help me retrieve knives and bring me snacks and water. My little green snake was never far from me either. What a strange little dwelling I'd found myself in and with such bizarre creatures for friends. But that was what they were becoming. The gossiping spirits and curious snakes were beginning to feel like home to me somehow.

So when I overheard Clara whisper to Edith about Red stopping by for a visit, I ducked behind a row of skull planters to eavesdrop. Who was Red? But the ghosts only floated out of earshot, passing through the stone walls and foliage as if they were nothing but mist. That made eavesdropping on entire conversations very difficult, I was learning. I'd gathered twenty half clues belonging to a variety of subjects, and I never quite knew if one thing was related to another. If only ghosts would stay in one spot.

After packing my knives, I bounded up the cobblestone steps and into the manor, looking around for a visitor or signs of company. Strange there had been no horse outside. Maybe Red had walked from town?

"Where would a dark mistress of evil take her guest?" I asked my green snake as he circled around my wrist. The little thing had grown on me. As I turned a corner, Paul floated out from a painting, making me jump. "Someday I'll get used to that," I breathed as he apologized for scaring me.

"Can I help you find something, Mistress Poesy?"

Not wanting to admit that I'd been listening in on ghost gossip, I simply said, "I'm looking for Lady Venom."

Paul rubbed the back of his neck. "She is indisposed at the moment. Perhaps I can help you? Would you like a snack? Arthur made some delightful lemon bars this morning."

His translucent arms ushered me back the way I came, which told me everything I needed to know. "Is someone here visiting?" I pressed, searching his expression.

Giving a nervous smile, he dodged the subject. "Visitors aren't entirely uncommon here, mistress."

Another burst of laughter echoed down the hall. "Then I'll go say hi." I smiled sanguinely and spun around the ghost's shoves. "But please do save me a lemon bar. Arthur's treats are the best."

The old ghost's worried grumbles of protest faded behind me as I sprinted down the hall, turning the knob and stumbling into what looked to be a tearoom or a dressing room. Dozens of sewing mannequins with pins sticking out of lavish garments cluttered the space, and hats hung on the walls like wearable decor. Lady Venom sat at a tiny round table, pausing her teacup mid-sip when she noticed me enter.

Her companion turned, her hair a red as deep as a ruby stone and her skin as white as the porcelain teacup she clutched. The corner of her mouth lifted in a predacious grin. The light glinted off her pronounced fang in a way that froze me in place as she purred. "Bas, this must be the new mistress you've been telling me about. Hello, Poesy. I'm Ezmerelda, and I've been dying to meet you."

CHAPTER FOURTEEN

THE WOMAN'S MOVEMENTS WERE quick yet as graceful as those of a deadly feline as she rose and slinked toward me. My mouth dried as her crimson gaze swept over me. "Well, well, well, the new mistress. What a winsome delight she is, Bas. I can see why you're so taken with her. Though"—she twirled a lock of my hair around her finger—"you never mentioned this delightful curly strawberry blond hair."

My cheeks heated as porcelain clinked and Lady Venom stood. "Red, darling. It's impolite to speak as if she's not standing right in front of you." Alabaster lifted the corner of her mouth, joining her friend. "And I do believe my letters detailed Poesy's beauty just fine."

She'd written letters about me? I could have fainted from that alone, but having both of their eyes on me was indeed making me dizzy.

"I'm Ezmerelda, or Ez, or The Red Vamp —"

Lady Venom cleared her throat. "Come, have some tea, bellflower." Putting a firm hand on my lower back, she guided me away from her friend, who regarded me very much like a kitten watches a canary. I took Lady Venom's seat, and she poured me a teacup of chamomile-scented warmth. As I sipped, I watched Ezmerelda spin about the room, dressed in a bright red corset and a billowing white skirt. Everything about her was a colorful contrast to my shadowy and reserved lady. Who watched on with amusement and supplied the most wicked banter that had me giggling in my seat.

"Would you look at this one." The fiery woman marveled at an indigo gown with delicate white lace. "It's outstanding. It must have taken you ages to sew."

"You sew?" I interrupted. Both women looked at me, and I found myself shrinking under their gaze again. They were each so unnaturally attractive it was hard to hold their stares for long without feeling completely inadequate under my frizzy curls and muddied loafers.

Lady Venom replied with a small voice. "A bit."

A flash of red appeared across from me, and I gasped. I hadn't even seen her move. Lady Venom shot her friend a stern stare, which Ezmerelda ignored, placing her chin on her knuckles and addressing me. "Bas is a master seamstress and far too humble. Why, everything you wear or see her wear is her creation."

My gaze snapped to the raven-haired beauty in the corner as she replaced a pin from a mannequin. "An old hobby," she dismissed without meeting my eyes.

Ez huffed, leaning back and taking a bite of scone. "So, Mistress Poesy, tell me about yourself. What in particular lured you into the clutches of my dear friend here? A siren's song, a long-forgotten curse, perhaps?" The woman in red raised an eyebrow over my shoulder, which I could only imagine was in response to Lady Venom's disapproving stare. Whoever this Ezmerelda was, she was untamed and wild. Much the contrast to the refinement and reservation I'd grown to expect from my lady. It was as if I could feel her nerves seeping into my back from where she stood close behind me. Alabaster was nervous. But why?

I'd witnessed her slaughter three men with nothing but glee, but for some reason, this woman made her hover around me and clutch her own palms. Another secret for me to uncover...

"Forgive my inquisitive companion." Lady Venom put her hands on my shoulders from behind, and I melted into her touch. "You don't have to share anything you don't want to."

"Oh, yes. Always feel free to ignore me," Ezmerelda agreed as she buttered another blueberry scone. "Did Arthur make these? He is a better baker than the devil himself."

My lady gripped my shoulders a bit at that, but I wasn't sure why.

"It's okay," I assured, looking up at her with a small smile before answering. "Actually both. A siren's song and a long-forgotten curse. You see, I grew up hearing stories in my town of Lady Venom. We'd hear the screams at night. We all knew men who went missing..." I fiddled with my teacup, glad that I could not see Alabaster's face as I spoke. "And the thought of a woman so powerful, so feared... it certainly enticed me."

"And the curse?" Ez cocked her head, now frozen and not tinkering with food or tea. I preferred the tinkering, as the undivided attention and my reflection in her crimson eyes were unnerving, to say the least.

"The curse, I suppose, was men. At least, the men who came around for the bidding. I was bought by Lord Harkness, and instead of dying by his hand, I thought it better to die by a more beautiful pair of hands." I planted my palms atop Lady Venom's as they still rested on my shoulders. My heart jumped when her thumb began softly stroking my pinky.

"Huh." Red patted her mouth with a napkin. "Want me to take care of him?"

"No," Lady Venom answered before I'd even surmised what the woman was asking. "I have other plans for Lord Harkness."

I looked up. "What plans?"

Ezmerelda was standing by the door before I'd realized she'd left the table. She was too unnaturally fast. "Tea and meeting your mistress have been delightful. I'll show myself to my room." As her red hair bounced behind her, she grabbed the indigo dress. "This one's mine until Marigold steals it. We'll talk again soon, Poesy."

And with that, the enigmatic woman breezed out the door, leaving silence in her stormy wake. I was fighting to sort through my thoughts and emotions when Lady Venom knelt beside me and took my face in her grip, pinching my cheeks as if I were a child.

She demanded my attention on her crystal blue gaze, and I would have given it without force, but the touch was nice, too.

"You are never to be alone with Ezmerelda. Do you understand?"

Holding her wrist, I tried to push her away, but she tightened her hold. "I *don't* understand, actually," I argued.

"You aren't meant to. All you should know and do is what I ask. Remember? Being my mistress means doing whatever I require of you. And for now, that is that you are never near her unsupervised."

Finally, I shoved her hand off. "Fine," I huffed, crossing my arms.

"Fine," she mirrored, standing and smoothing her verdant dress. Wishing me a nice afternoon, she left me alone among her sewing. They were lovely, each embroidered with lace or tulle. Each could have belonged to a different mood, a different persona or hidden depth of the seamstress who'd crafted them. And there I was, sitting among them. Just another fine thing, a fabric-stuffed dummy. Made for dress-up, for gawking or flaunting before being stashed away and left in the dark.

Maybe the title of mistress wasn't such a compliment after all.

CHAPTER FIFTEEN

I SPENT THE NEXT two days in my room. Mostly sulking, reading, and avoiding the creepy women of the house. Oddly, that didn't include the ghosts. Edith stopped by to check my forehead for a fever and give me sideways glances, clearly not believing my excuse of just being tired. Meg misted through my door with a steady stream of snacks and thoughtfully curated gossip.

"I'm not sure how they met, but they've been friends for ages. She never stays long. In fact, her bag is already packed." Meg fluffed my bed's pillows. "She's peculiar but polite. Well, aside from her odd desires."

"What odd desires?" I asked, pulling my blanket down and meeting the glassy eyes of my ghost friend. "Meg, I know you know more than you're saying."

With a pained expression, she folded a throw blanket. "There's much that is not mine to tell, Poesy, or I would. Trust me."

With a sigh, I slumped back into the plush comforts of the canopy bed. "Ez is better than me. Lady Venom likes her better, doesn't she?"

The thought had pained me for days. I imagined walking the halls and catching them kissing and wanted to throw myself off the balcony with jealousy. I was just the toy. Red was the permanent fixture. The equal to Lady Venom in both beauty and mystique. How could I compete with that? Where we were all three perfectly curvaceous, I was shorter than both of them and more like a doll, while they wore their ample breasts, their soft middles, and their supple thighs like entrancing gardens meant to entice, to touch, to sample. My body invited no such thing. Their aura was sex and seduction. Mine was, at best, a passing glance.

Meg grabbed my blanket and opened my curtains, making me hiss at my lack of covering and the bright sunlight. "Is a sunflower more beautiful than a daisy? All flowers just bloom. Beauty does not compete; it simply flourishes. Like you need to. Come on, get up."

I glared at my friend. "How old are you?"

"Twenty." She smiled, floating through a desk chair. "Plus a hundred or so."

A small laugh huffed from my chest as I pulled myself out of bed. "No wonder you're so wise."

"Go for a walk, pick some cherries, stab a bag of flour. You'll feel better."

Slipping on a lightweight sage green gown, I rubbed the fabric tenderly, pressing my fingers in the indents of thread. Lady Venom had sewn this. She'd created it from her mind and crafted it with her hands. So much talent and artistry existed beneath her steely surface.

The late spring air held a promise of summer as I traipsed through one of the estate's eerie gardens. In the misty dew, tiny white skull-shaped flowers bobbed beneath bumble bees and long strands of ebony snap dragons swayed as if they were waving a hello to the bronze rattlesnakes that currently weaved beneath them. Lady Venom had warned me the garden was toxic. Like I'd needed the warning. Everything in this place was some creative and tragic invitation to death. Beyond the garden was a willow tree, and its long canopy branches invited me into hiding as a drizzly rain began to fall. Spreading the quilt Meg had sent me with, I sat under its protection as the rain softly fell. A branch rattled, and when I glanced up, expecting a snake or a squirrel, I yelped at a flash of crimson dropping in front of me.

"Perfect day for tree-climbing," Ezmerelda explained as I caught my breath. "The trees here are particularly chatty, too. But dodging the snakes is a real pain."

"I don't understand anything you just said." I scooted back, as if I could hide behind the trunk of the willow. But it was no use; I was caged in by the vines, the rain, and the red-haired temptress before me.

With a melodic laugh, she stroked a vine. "You're in love with her."

My breath caught in my chest. "I—I don't know what you mean—"

"Humans are so shy about expressing their feelings, so peculiar. As if you have all the time in the world." She sighed. "A blessing that you do not. But even still, why not shout it from the treetops?"

My brain fumbled around the way she regarded me as *human*, as if she were *not*. "Even if I did love her, I'm just her mistress. Her captive."

"I don't believe that, and I don't believe that *you* believe that either. But if you admitted it, it could be a powerful thing for her."

"Do you... are you in love with her?" I swallowed, jealousy churning in my gut at the question. But something about the rain, the coziness of our seclusion, lowered my defenses.

Ez grinned, tossing her long, un-frizzed scarlet hair over her shoulder. "Bas and I will always share love, but not the kind you're thinking of. When you're as old as I am, you learn after a century or two that enduring friendships are far more valuable than fleeting lovers." Her ruby eyes lit up at the sight of my blanching. *Centuries?* "I do adore women. Prefer them, even," she continued, spinning around the willow like a dance. "But alas, I am unfortunately vexed with love for a man. Though I'll never let him know it."

This admission should not have brought about the relief it did. It should have sent me running for so many reasons. But my petty and simple soul delighted in the awareness that Ez was not after my lady.

"What are you?" I narrowed my gaze, my attention flicking back to her pointed teeth.

She giggled. "As much as I would adore watching my friend combust at the knowing that I told you, I'll continue leaving you cryptic little clues until you piece it all together. Ah, to be there the moment that you do... but no, I'll let her have that experience with you, mistress."

In that moment, as the rain picked up, I decided that, despite her unsettling movements and words, I liked Ezmerelda. She was a good friend to Lady Venom. She wished me goodbye with a kiss on my hand, and departed. As she did, a crash of thunder brought another visitor.

"I thought I told you not to be alone with her," my lady's voice scolded when she parted the vines. Her hair was wet from the rain and her black gown clung to her body as if she'd been standing outside the tree the whole time.

"Eavesdropping?" I accused, standing and crossing my arms.

She stepped forward. "You'd know a thing or two about that, wouldn't you? How many ghost conversations are you still attempting to string together, Poesy?"

My mouth dropped in indignation as I wobbled on my heels. "Yes. Well, sorry I'm not a good little mistress. Even though I've played the part as a dress-up doll and plaything my entire life, I wasn't prepared to do it for you, too."

A flash of hurt swept her gorgeous features as a bolt of lightning illuminated the swaying vines. She stepped closer. So close I could feel the heat from her body on my damp skin. "If you want to leave, go." She gestured away from me. "By all means, I'll draw your horse."

I didn't know why, but that comment stabbed a shard of hurt right through my chest. "Just like that? What happened to being your captive?"

Lady Venom's breath came out in a puff of smoke from the cool air. "If you don't want me, then I will release you. I've never been one to keep the rules."

I swallowed down the tears welling in my throat as I leaned back against the tree, daring my hands to reach out and hold her waist. "Alabaster, I want you deeply, and that is the beginning and end of everything."

Her berry-colored lips parted in a small gasp before she moved closer, pressing her hips to mine. "Really? Please, don't tease me, bellflower."

Her hands cupped my face as she searched my eyes. Pulling her hips closer, I nodded. "Don't send me away. Ever."

"Never," she agreed before pressing her lips to mine. "You belong to me," she breathed between kisses, and the heat in my stomach dropped between my thighs.

"And you're mine," I murmured, parting her lips with my tongue and slipping it inside her mouth, finding the forked taste of her. A moan escaped my throat as she pinned me against the tree, breathing heavily into my kiss. She'd never displayed such passion *with* me. She'd only elicited it *from* me. That moment felt so raw and very much like a gift.

My lady tugged me forward and spun me around, guiding us to the ground so I was leaning against her breasts. She wrapped my hair around her wrist and tugged my head back onto her shoulder. "You look at me while I watch you. And do exactly as I say. Do you understand?"

I tried to nod, but her grip was too tight. "Yes," I breathed as she pulled my gown up to my waist, exposing my naked thighs and wet panties.

Those crystal eyes—not just blue, purely clear, like those of a supernatural predator—glinted in approval. "Good. Now remove your panties and take your pointer finger and circle your clit slowly."

Inhaling sharply, I did as I was told, wiggling out of my underwear and inching my hand down my core, noticing her gaze sink to where my finger obeyed.

"Good girl, Poesy. Now spread your legs wider. I want to see all of you as you touch yourself for me."

I was spread bare and at her mercy, the way she wanted it. My knees rested against hers, and my hips warmed against her thighs. I tilted my chin down, begging for a look at her beautiful body. With a hard yank of my hair, I yelped, and my head was back in the crook of her neck. "Only I get to watch you tease your perfect little pussy. Pick up the pace now. Go a little harder for me. That's it," she purred in my ear. "Oh, you're divine, my sweet bellflower."

As my release built, her voice broke my trance again. "Now slip two fingers inside. Move them in and out. I want to hear it. Let me hear how wet you are for me, how much you want me. Make the nectar from your sweet cunt sing my name, Poesy."

"Alabaster, you're so lyrically dirty," I panted a small tease, letting my fingers push inside my wet opening. I was but her puppet on a string, I'd do anything she asked, and she knew it. "I want your touch instead," I begged, coaxing the sounds she wanted from my wetness.

Her head tilted as she watched my show, and her berry purple lips parted slightly. "Come for me now, Poesy. I want it to gush, to drench your palm. Can you do that for me, my sweet?" She gave my hair a tug and wrapped her arm around my ribs, letting her thumb stroke the underside of my breast through the thin fabric of my gown. "That's it. Come for me."

That refined, seductive voice shattered my orgasm onto my slick fingers. While my walls still tightened around them, Lady Venom's hold softened in my hair while her other grip met my wrist. She pulled my hand up and smirked, knowing I was watching her, entirely enraptured by her splendor. Her sharp, forked tongue extended. It was the same as mine, apart from the divot in the middle, I wondered if she was born with it or if she truly was becoming like one of her snakes. I wouldn't ask. I couldn't form words. All I could do was gasp at the feel of its apex as it wrapped around my fingers. Closing her eyes, she groaned, taking my two digits into her mouth and sucking, cleaning my taste off my skin.

"You just may be my favorite flavor, Poesy Foxglove." She caressed the back of my neck as I leaned against her.

I giggled, feeling my body relax. "You have so many names for me, and somehow I like them all."

"There are so many different parts of you, my dear. So many wondrous qualities and interests that haven't been tended. I find myself adoring every sprout, every dark bloom of you."

And from that moment onward, I never felt like a garment of hers, ever again.

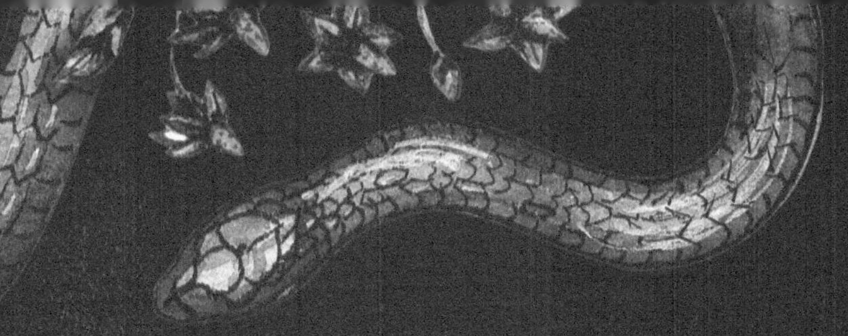

CHAPTER SIXTEEN

Our touches transformed into idle, reverent sweeps of skin as Alabaster traced my arms and I circled her knees. I snuggled into her embrace as we lounged under the willow vines as the storm petered past.

"I didn't seek Ezmerelda out. She found me," I confessed, breaking the silence, still ruminating on the red-haired woman's earlier words and Lady Venom's eagerness to keep me from them.

She continued tracing my arms. "I know."

"Ezmerelda isn't... human, is she?" Thunder rumbled in the distance, and I was sure my lady would brush me off, but she answered as simply and normally as ever.

"No, she is not."

"Is that why you're friends?" It was a cowardly way of asking, *are you not-human, too?*

"Keep rubbing my knees," she purred sweetly, and I smiled, not realizing I'd stopped. "Red understands me. Though what I am... is worse than what she is."

Shaking my head, I blew out a breath. "You and the ghosts are so skilled at your non-answers."

"Skill comes with age, little foxglove. Shall I show you what more I'm skilled at?"

Those words and her breath on my neck were all it took for the fire in my lower belly to reignite. "Yes, please," I whispered, leaning back and offering her my lips again.

With a soft kiss, she responded. "Go, have a meal, get out of these wet clothes, and meet me in my room."

"Yes, my lady." No hesitation existed between her orders and my obedience, and she smiled again. Upon closer look, her pointer teeth were not as long as Ezmerelda's were, and it made me believe that they weren't the same after all. What made them understand each other, and what sort of non-humans were they? I'd heard stories of witches and devils my entire life. Somehow, Lady Venom seemed like all and none of them at once. How would I ever sort out which she was? And would it even matter when I did?

We took separate paths home, but I always felt her eyes on me. She seemed to prefer a degree of separation, an apartness that made me want her all the more. But little by little, like single drops of rain on orchid petals, that distance was dissipating. With a kiss, with a look, with the command for more awaiting me in her room. I felt triumphant, like a small barrier between us had been broken down. Maybe the red sharp-toothed girl had helped with that. And for that, I vowed to thank Ez someday.

Stopping to pick a blackberry, I put a hand to my mouth to cover a gasp as a trickle of blood ran down the branch. Alabaster paused behind me and I turned, "No, don't look," I urged.

With a soft smile she joined my side, putting a tender hand on my lower back. "Black mambas are one of the deadliest snakes in the realm. But they're curious and prideful." She reached past me and eased the dead serpent's body off the branch.

"What happened to it?" I swallowed, finding that I hated the sight of its death. No matter my feelings of fear when I'd arrived, the snakes had grown to be some sort of strange comfort. Their benevolent presence was tucked into every crevice of this place. And also, they reminded me of her, and anything that reminded me of my lady brought me joy.

Clutching the long, limp rope of a body, Lady Venom glided to a large orange pitcher-shaped bloom. "The snakes and the birds are at war. Looks as if the crows won a battle today." She sighed. "Either way, the carnivorous plants get a meal."

I stroked between her shoulder blades, then laced my fingers with hers as the plant slowly swallowed its victim. Her mouth was a straight line for a moment before she exhaled and gave my hand a squeeze.

When she pulled away and ascended the stone steps, she looked back over her shoulder and gave me a wry smile. "Ezmerelda's known as the Red Vampiress. Tales of her are most legendary."

"W-what?" I asked, my breath catching in my throat as I halted at the bottom of the stairs, looking up at my mysterious lover, my mouth agape.

"Red is a vampire," she said plainly. "See you in my room soon." Alabaster gave a short chuckle before blowing me a kiss and disappearing into the manor. My blood chilled as the pieces clicked into place. I'd just been alone with a... vampire. And if Ezmerelda was a blood thirsty creature of the night... what did that make Alabaster?

CHAPTER SEVENTEEN

SECURING A SNUG PAIR of brown trousers, I buttoned up a lacy pink blouse. These clothes weren't for throwing knives or riding Penny. These were for drawing my lady's gaze to my intense curves. Frequently, I'd caught her stare drifting to my thick hips and rounded thighs, so I was sure to accentuate them in the most form-fitting getup possible. I separated my light red curls so they bounced atop my breasts.

I surveyed myself in the mirror, finding a different girl staring back at me than the one who'd arrived. My freckles were darker, my cheeks rosier with life and health. My body both strong and on display. My time in the sun had lightened my hair from auburn to strawberry and dusted new freckles on my nose and arms. My looks were still nothing compared to Lady Venom's. Where she was a brooding night sky, I was an orange and pink sunrise. But together, we were life itself. What life should be, at least. A life I wished every girl back in my town awaiting their bidding could experience. Days filled with mystery, hauntings, and passion. A lover who encouraged me to find out who I was, on my own terms, and delighted in that unfolding.

She was pensive and reclusive, and maybe a bit strange, but I couldn't imagine anyone better for me than Lady Venom. But could

I be the same for her? Could I pierce her walls covered in snakes and vines?

The fragrant bath lingered on my skin, leaving me smelling like citrus sweetness, and my heart fluttered as I reached the west wing of the manor. It was the first time she'd invited me to her room, and my nerves were a jumble of tangled ribbons in my throat. Deciding against knocking, I closed her ebony door behind me and admired the dim, black candlelit room. It was as mysterious and eerie as she was but with an inexpressible warmth that made me want to stay.

"Hello, bellflower." Her sultry coo from the corner of the room sent chills down my spine.

"My lady." I whispered an already breathless reply as she slinked into view. The sight of her warmed my middle and sent my mind into a frenzy of desire. A thin silk and wickedly short black nightgown was all Lady Venom needed to entrance me entirely. Her long, straight, deep purple hair cascaded down her exposed back, and I could make out her hard nipples through the thin fabric.

She quirked her lips. "Tell me what you're thinking."

"That I could get lost in the maze of your body forever," I breathed as she stood in front of me. Not being able to resist, I skimmed my hands from her waist, following the line outward to her supple hips.

"You, Poesy..." She grabbed my waist and pulled me flush to her body. Dipping, she planted a kiss on my neck. "Bellflower, foxglove, love... your body is poetry."

With a deep sigh, I leaned into her and lifted my palms up the slick fabric of her ribs, greedy for her full breasts. Pulling back, she took my wrists. "This shade of pink matches your delicious little pussy, and these pants," she purred, unbuttoning them and easing them down. "Remove your clothes and get on the bed."

Excitement rippled with a mixture of disappointment as I undid my top while she watched hungrily. "Would you let me look at you?" I asked, dropping my blouse to the ground and letting my heavy breasts drop freely. "Could I taste and touch you, too? I want to make you feel as good as you make me feel." Her red lips parted as she watched me move closer. I fiddled with the tiny strap of her nightgown. "Please?" I pleaded, sensing she was wrestling with her answer.

Sucking in a breath, she traced a circle on the soft dip between my hip and thighs. "There's much you don't know about me, bellflower. About who I am, what I am, what I've done..."

I dropped my lips to her neck and sucked the sweet skin there lightly. "If you're a vampire, like your friend, I don't care." I tilted my head. "Here, drink all you'd like."

Her grin was wicked, and her grip tightened on my hips. "Darling, if I were a vampiress, you'd have long been sucked dry."

"Then a witch? It doesn't matter to me, Alabaster. The ghosts, the snakes, I love it all."

"Do you?" Her voice quivered slightly as I peppered soft kisses along her collarbone. It was the most she'd ever let me give, and the taste of her was addicting. "I do."

"I loved a mistress once, so much that I told her, and then she left... terrified of me. Disgusted," she breathed.

Halting my kissing, I held her waist and found her crystal gaze. Gently, I tucked her hair behind her ear. "I'm not your mistress anymore."

"No?" She cocked an eyebrow.

"I'm more. At least, I think I am."

"You are," she confirmed, biting her lip.

A small giggle shook my shoulders. "You slaughter men with ease, yet the thought of sharing about yourself has you trembling."

"The latter is inarguably more terrifying."

Chuckling, I took her hand and led her to the black expanse of her bed. The place we'd shared cherry pie and quiet comfortability. We lay on our sides, me naked, and my lady considering how much to reveal, both inwardly and out. I'd coax her for as long as it took. I wanted her, all of her.

Leaning forward, I brought my lips to hers. She accepted my kiss, letting my tongue find hers and press into the forked wedge in the middle. "Where does this come from?"

"How about…" She inched her hand over my belly button and down to my sex. She tugged gently at the tuft of hair there before slipping a slender finger lightly into my slit. "For every orgasm you give me, I'll give you one thing you want."

"Anything I want?" I asked, tilting my hips into her touch. "Questions answered?"

"Yes," she purred, finding my wetness pooling and hissing lightly. "So wet for me already, bellflower."

Her fingers worked in a figure eight motion, painting my arousal around my clit before swirling back down to my opening for more. My first release was quick with passion as I bucked against her digits.

With a small laugh, she chided. "I think you rushed that one."

"Just a little," I admitted, cupping her jaw. "Now give me your monster, Alabaster Baudelaire."

Something flashed behind her eyes, something primal and lust filled. And in a swift movement, she pinned me to the bed. She straddled me, her nightgown ruching around her waist, revealing her thick thighs and the smallest peek of her cunt. But it was her eyes shining against her pale skin and dark hair that rendered me speechless beneath her.

"You want the monster?" she asked, her voice taking on a new and echoey cadence that numbed my bones.

"I want it all," I whimpered. "Give it to me, Lady Venom."

Her sharp pointed incisors gleamed in the candlelight as she opened her mouth and unfurled her black forked tongue. Confusion dried my mouth. It hadn't been that long before, had it? It was long and exactly like a serpent. I'd seen it black, but also pink. Though now I wondered how it could change so drastically. Then she moved, slinking down my middle and spreading my knees apart. "You're afraid," she echoed. "I taste it."

"Y-you taste my fear?"

"I taste your every emotion, my love. Though you're also aroused, curious, and"—she flicked her tongue down my slit—"feeling deeply for me," she revealed.

"Those are true," I whined as she licked my clit. "Tell me," I urged.

"You want to know what I am? Look at me. Now."

Lifting my head, I took in her eyes. They were stark white now, with no pupils. Her black tongue was long and thick, and I watched as she used it to circle my opening. "You're so beautiful," I whimpered, knowing I was being devoured by a monster and loving every moment of it.

"I am an archdemoness, Poesy," she echoed, not giving me time to react before thrusting her tongue inside me. I cried out, the pleasure, the awareness of the revelation shocking through me along with her thick, throbbing tongue.

"A—a demoness?" I moaned.

She purred, vibrating against my walls, leading me to another shattering orgasm as her tongue twisted, wet and thorough in its assault. Drinking every bit of my wet release. When she finally pulled out, she rose onto her knees. "An archdemon. I am the worst of them all. The strongest and most wretchedly cursed of all the demons of hell, Poesy. Associating with me means sure and certain death for you."

I rose onto my shaking knees, my slick inner thighs rubbing together with wetness. I took her hands and searched her glassy white stare. "I'll take it," I breathed. "Give me your death, because I was never truly alive until I met you."

Our kiss collided with ferocious velocity then, and she growled something lithe and feral. My hands tangled in her hair, and she pinned me back on the bed. Her silk lingerie twisted in my grip as I tugged it up and over her cleavage. To my delight, she didn't stop me. Sitting up, she peeled it off, allowing me full view of her breathtaking body. Where we were both curvaceous and full, there was an art to her body that I'd never beheld before.

"Alabaster," I breathed, my eyes wrenching from the soft way her thighs pressed over my hips, the *S*-shape of her sides, like snow-covered hills I wanted to frolic in forever. "You're so beautiful it's physically painful."

With a wicked gleam in her eye, she knelt to suck at my nipple. "Only a very particular type of girl is enchanted by something as nightmarish as a demon. But I'm so happy you are. And now that I have you, I'm never letting you go."

"Good," I sighed. "I'll be your captive forever." I inched my finger between her lips and stroked her tongue. "Tie me up with this anytime, my lady."

"Don't tempt me," she purred, shoving a knee against my pussy, making me gasp as she straddled my leg. "Move your hips for me, bellflower."

I did as I was told, tilting forward and back until my wetness slicked her and my clit glided against her soft thigh. "Please, use me, too," I begged, raising my leg to prod against her warm sex.

"I'm not one to take orders from anyone," she breathed. "But I'll make an exception this time." And then she began to ride my thigh. My back arched, and a moan escaped me as I took in the sight of her. The beauty of her breasts bouncing with the movements, the feel of her nectar painting my thigh with her pleasure. "Yes. That's it, bellflower. Come with your archdemoness."

Her thumbs flicked against my nipples, and I leaned forward, taking hers into my mouth, groaning at the sweet texture of them as I sucked. The most beautiful sigh left her lips as she tilted her head back, still riding my leg. I held her hips for leverage and bucked against her, finding the most brilliant friction on her soft skin until finally, despite my best efforts to draw it out, I moaned around her nipple as my bliss fragmented to my core. And to my rapture, so did my lady's. Her moan was a melody of surrender, of love and trust, as she so beautifully broke against me, her juices running down my inner thigh and hip.

When she got up, my breathing was still fighting to catch up with the moment. "No. Come back." I reached for her as she walked to a chest of drawers.

With a small giggle, she bent, looking through the drawer for something. "I'm not done with you yet, my dear."

My attention caught on her perfect peach of an ass, and my mouth watered. When would I get a taste of her? She'd now been naked and racked with pleasure on my skin, and instead of pride, I only felt insatiable lust for more. Lady Venom was my cruel and demonic addiction, and I couldn't have been happier with that.

Something long and thick rested in her palms, and she carried it over, sashaying her hips in a hypnotic way that had me eager for more of her already. The item was clear and long and... I sat up on my elbows. "Is that a—"

"Yes, it is," she replied, grinning wickedly and drawing out the *ssss* with a flick of her forked tongue. The serpent queen had not yet had her fill, and this object had me both terrified and intrigued. "This is a silicone mold of my favorite snake... and I'm going to fuck you with it."

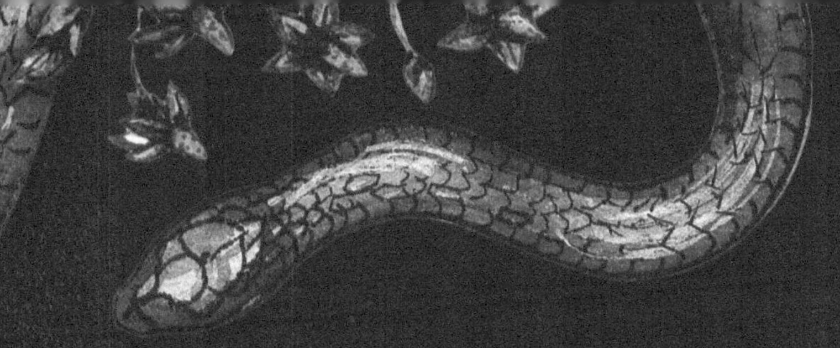

CHAPTER EIGHTEEN

A COUGH OF SURPRISE made me scoot away, my back pressing against the tall, ornate black headboard. "You made a statue of your favorite snake?" I asked in shock. "And you want to…"

Her pointed teeth gleamed, giving away every bit the demoness she was. It all made sense now. A demoness. An *archdemoness*, which sounded even scarier… and hotter than just a regular, you know, *demon*.

Alabaster petted its fanned head. "A king cobra, or shall I say *queen* cobra. She lived to be twenty-five, and I named her Sylvie. Remarkable reptile." She sat on the bed next to my knees, showing me the details ingrained in her creation. "When she died, I had a ghost mold this for me so I could keep her memory in my room. Though time went by, and I discovered other uses for the little replica."

"N-not so little!" I winced, noticing the thickest part of the object was bigger than my bicep.

"Sylvie would have approved. She was the most amorous creature, mating with every male and female serpent she could find. Now…" she purred, holding the toy by the fanned head and waving it along the bed, imitating a real snake, kissing up my ankle. I jerked, squealing and pulling up a sheet, eliciting lyrical laughter from my lady.

"Oh, pretty little Poesy. Where is that sweet cunt?" she hissed, her tone echoing with hell again as she crawled alongside her creation. With a swift movement, the sheet disappeared, and she was between my legs again, pushing my knees apart. "I want to watch you take this. I want to watch your pussy stretch and expand as I pump it in and out of you."

I tried to pull my knees back together, but she only held them open. "Deep breaths. You can do it. You're such a good girl, bellflower. You can take me and my serpent here, can't you?"

"I don't know," I hesitated, but I was already breathless and lying back, offering myself to her again.

She licked her lips, and her eyes rolled back. "Fear. Oh, Poesy, your fear tastes delectable. Like warm cherries in the sun."

"You're frightening," I admitted. "But I'm learning to enjoy the sensation of it."

"Good girl." She lowered, unfurling her tongue and flicking it with a slap against my tender pussy. "Good little human girl. Good little captive mistress."

"Yes," I whined, wiggling my hips nervously. She worked at my clit with her hypnotic tongue for what seemed like ages. Coaxing me to release, only to pull back and watch me float back to earth on a wet writhe of black sheets. The long, clear toy blended into the dark expanse of the bed, waiting to strike like any real snake might.

Noticing me eyeing it, she held it up again. It was long, so impossibly long, and thick. Taking my hand, she made me touch it, feel the protruding bone of its spine along the middle of its thick body. "Feel? Soft but firm. And this little peak here feels most pleasurable once it's inside. Do you trust me, bellflower?"

"With everything I have," I answered without hesitation, feeling my fear dissipate slightly as my walls clenched in anticipation of what the toy could feel like inside me.

"Perfect," she hissed, crawling up my body and capturing my lips with hers. Biting my lower lip, she eased the object against my opening. I entwined my leg with hers and wrapped my arms around her as she watched my face, nudging the literal head inside. A cry of stretch and pleasure fled my throat and gargled against her serpentine smile. "That's it. Oh, look at you taking it for me, Poesy. Your cunt is so greedy for whatever I offer. Even something as depraved as this, isn't it?"

I nodded, knowing it was sickeningly true as she pushed in another inch and sighed with satisfaction, leaning back to look at me. The head buried and long tail flowing out of me. Gasping at the erotic and wicked sight, she smiled, her chin still glistening with me. "So perfect," she cooed. "Look at you, little snake whore." I groaned, liking the sound of that and the way she began to work the toy inside me. "I wonder..." Lady Venom mused, pulling it slowly out. "Ah, that lovely shade of red."

Startling, I looked up in time to see the toy's head brushed with blood before Lady Venom took it into her mouth and sucked it off. "Delicious," she groaned. "Oh, you bled so well, giving me all your cherry delight. My favorite dessert and flavor of all. Now, take it harder."

"Oh my god," I moaned as she pushed it back in, harder now, thrusting in and out at a mad pace. "Ride with me," I begged, my hips moving on their own now. "Please, Alabaster, please."

She was breathless, too, her cheeks rosy with flush of want, and she obeyed, straddling the long spine of silicone where it burrowed into my pussy. After shifting her hold to its underside, I reached down to help, my hand cupping her knuckles. "Together," I breathed.

It was logistic. It was sexual in intent and desire. But it was also a plea, an offering. Wholly a declaration. *Together? Me and you?* And maybe it was my imagination, but her answering smile was pure dark love when she repeated in agreement. "Together."

We moved the long thickness slower now, groaning as we learned our dance with each other. The top of her sex brushed against mine as we used the extension between us. Her hips moved back and forth as mine inched up and down. Our pace marrying, becoming tuned. We were one. The Lady and her taken mistress. The demoness and the damned. But also just two women who loved each other.

That last thought, swirled with the darker ones, is what sent me tumbling into the heaviest and longest orgasm of my life. My scream echoed through the room, and Lady Venom didn't take her eyes off me as she mirrored my bliss. Her own release racked her body, her wetness blooming from her beautiful cunt and dripping into mine, flooding me with her. As multiple rounds of ecstasy bolted us together, I pulled her down, demanding that her kiss drink my screams of pleasure.

Lady Venom wasn't a vampire. No, she was far more wicked. A figment of terror hid beneath every aspect of her being. And I was irrevocably bewitched by her darkness.

I pushed her off, smoothing the toy away. She lay beneath me, her usual trepidation now a wary facade, fucked away just the way I hoped it would be. "I'm going to taste you now. Oh, please let me, Alabaster. I've dreamed of nothing else."

Her gorgeous breasts rose and fell as her full lips parted. "You may."

Those words on her demoness tongue sent a thrill of heat between my legs. Nowhere close to sated—in fact, hungrier than ever—I got on my knees between her thighs. I kneeled before my queen as she watched me with hooded eyes and long, dark lashes. Her hair was messed up and spilled around her pillow in shimmers of deep purple. Her lily pale skin glowed in the candlelight, contrasting against the black bedding. "I could stay here and look at you forever," I murmured in awe.

"My legs don't spread for only looking," she teased. "Please me, taste me, drink me, mistress."

Oh, yes, call me mistress in bed. "Yes, lady." I lifted her ankle and kissed it, trailing my tongue down the arch of her foot. "Archdemoness," I sighed. Her toes wiggled before I sucked them into my mouth, reveling in the taste of her skin. She exhaled as I made my way to her other leg, repeating the process before licking up her calf and the plush flesh of her inner thighs. Her legs came to rest over my shoulders as I palmed her dripping pussy, stroking the incredibly soft diamond of hair there. She trembled as I spread her wide and took in the deep pink of her, like rose petals misted with dew. Wiggling her hips, she nudged forward, and I giggled. "If you think I'm going to rush this moment, you're mistaken."

But the whimper that left her throat when my finger dipped inside her begged me to take her hard and fast. I would another time, but this first moment, this offering she gave, would be savored with all the reverence worthy of my lady demoness.

Her walls were silky smooth as I caressed my fingers in and out. I could have watched her writhe and wandered among her moans for a lifetime, but my mouth watered in thirst, in greedy hunger to have her flavor grace my mouth. I lowered, swiping her hard clit with my tongue and letting out a whimper of my own. Devils, her taste was a poison garden all my own. Floral with the innocence of flowers and the sharp edge of death. I could become drunk with ease and never grow tired of her. Flicking my tongue up and down and back and forth, I glided over her, and my fingers were squeezed tighter and tighter by her cunt. Her groans and whimpers turned frantic as her hands tangled in the wild curls of my hair. She pulled me closer, burying my face in the sweet darkness of her center, pushing her wetness against my cheeks, pulling my nose against her. It was sweet, heavenly torture, and I savored every moment of her smell, her taste, her silky walls constricting around my fingers as they pumped inside her. My lady came undone in the most glorious and breathtaking way. Screaming the melody written by my tongue and forced through her cunt, to her lips, and into the ethers.

I didn't stop, couldn't stop, swallowing every new drop of her cum, feeling it drip warm down my chin. The flutters of her pussy palpated around my knuckles in a dance of passion.

And then she pulled at my hair, grabbing my shoulders and easing me up, pulling me on top of her. Breathless, she trailed the outline of my face, her touch tender. "These rosy, perfect, freckled cheeks... this glorious mouth..." I closed my eyes, leaning into her touch. "Now," she breathed, pulling my hips forward and slithering down, down beneath me. "Ride my face like the good little mistress you are."

"Ride your face?" Surprise and heat were evident in my words.

Moving between my thighs, her hair ribbons of raven velvet around my knees, she grinned and flicked out her black snake tongue. "Just like you rode the pillow, Poesy. Ride my face hard. I want to feel your thrusts on my lips. Mmm, I've been jealous of that goddamn pillow for weeks." She cupped my ass and dug her nails into my flesh, pulling me atop her. And without warning or preamble, her tongue was impaling me. My moan transformed into a quiver of inexpressible pleasure as her long demon tongue pushed in and out. It was long enough to curve outward and glide across my clit, too.

Then I don't know whether I began rocking my hips against her or if her hold made me move as her sharp fingers pricked my ass, but my rhythm burst into a frenetic back and forth. I was at first afraid of hurting her or smothering her, but as she moaned between my thick thighs and squeezed my plump ass, it seemed as if she wanted all I could give. So I gave it to her. Holding on to the headboard with both hands and leveraging my pelvis at the perfect angle, I bucked wildly against my demoness's long, forked tongue, hitting it just right, sending bolts of bliss shrieking throughout my entire soul. My opening full with bumpy wetness, my clit rocking against the flat of her tongue, the point of her chin, and the base of her nose. The sensations were overwhelming in the most earth shattering of ways.

"God!" I cried out, feeling tears streak against my face. Tears of passion, of electricity, of the metaphorical ribbon around my neck not only being cut, but burned in hell with my demoness. I was no man's, and I never would be. I would always and forever be her captive, her mistress. And somehow, I'd earn the favor of being her love, too. Lady Venom was mine, but even sweeter, Alabaster Baudelaire was mine. All of her. Every evil, mysterious, delectable inch. I would make her darkness, her ghosts, and her snakes my own. My pleasure would belong to my lady. And like a foolish man dying between the teeth of a snakebite, I died a slow and agonizing little death at the viper strike of my Lady Venom. A surge of venom throughout my body that I would never recover from—and I never wanted the antidote. Her venom could kill me slowly for the rest of time, and I'd lie naked at her feet in only the most blissful of wicked gratitude.

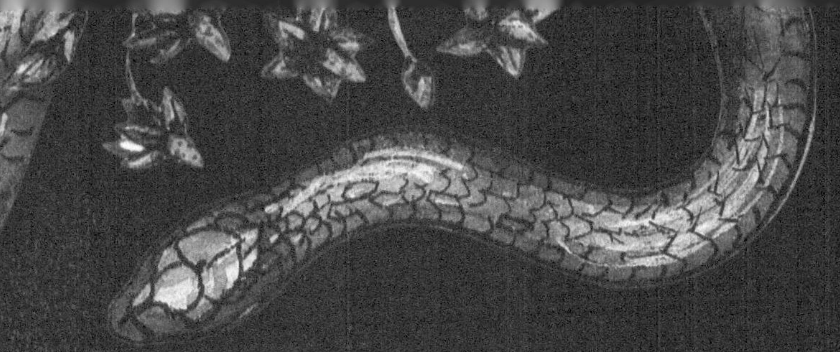

CHAPTER NINETEEN

My leg draped over her bare hips as I watched her chest rise and fall. My sleeping serpentine queen. Our rounds with the snake toy had intoxicated my mind into forgetting the question that plagued me when I awoke. It was possibly the most important one, the one whose answer I feared, though I felt I knew the answer from the worried tone of the ghosts' gossip.

Inhaling her soft hair, I nuzzled my lips to her ear. "Lady Venom. Alabaster. What happens when you kill seven men a year?"

She sucked in a breath. "You've pieced it together by now, dear. May as well say it."

"Do you die? Along with the ghosts?" How a demoness and already dead spirits could die again, I didn't know, but I didn't know the rules or workings of this new world.

She hummed, rolling over and kissing the edge of my jaw. "I do adore speaking of death first thing in the morning."

Giggling, I believed her word to not be a joke. My macabre madame.

"I was cursed by a devil long ago in a bargain I made out of desperation. Killing seven men is my mercy, my tamed bloodlust. If I surpass it, I will be forever locked in the depths of hell where I belong."

I swallowed, horrified. "You've killed too many for me already."

She shrugged a pale shoulder. "Hell does not concern me as much as leaving the spirits without a guardian. They find me, and I give them a home. A purpose outside a cemetery or graveyard or abandoned property. They are under my charge and bound to me the moment they decide to stay. Without me, they'd simply fade away. A fate they all avoid and dread for one reason or another."

I sat up, my head pounding. "And here I come, bringing men straight to your slaughter. I'm risking everyone's life. I'm—I'm a plague on this place."

Rising, Alabaster took my palms and kissed my wrists. Her lily white breasts were glorious in the easy morning light. "There always lie hidden pathways to salvation, even in the most haunted of woods."

Kissing her lips tenderly, I shook my head. "I have no idea what that means, but it sounds lovely on your tongue."

It was on the tip of my being, a declaration I wanted to say and feared in equal measure. *I love you.* Her crystal blue eyes glimmered with white, and I wondered if the demoness knew. If she tasted my devotion and my cowardice in not speaking it. "Stay just like this. I'll be right back," I whispered, crawling out of bed. Slipping into my trousers and buttoning my blouse, I left my lady tangled in black sheets, looking after me wistfully. Maybe the walk to the garden would make me brave.

That was it. I'd pick her a lovely bouquet of purple and black flowers, fetch breakfast from the kitchen, and then drop to my knees and devour her while murmuring I love yous against her honeyed cunt. Nothing less than everything would do for her. And I'd make it glorious and special, because she deserved it.

The blooms still watched me as I passed by, barefoot, stepping over several albino snakes as they scurried by. I even let my toes skim over the soft back of one, and it didn't flinch. They knew me now, and I knew them. They were each a part of my lady, and therefore I understood and admired them. My own little green garden friend wrapped around a blackberry bush. Kneeling, I plucked a small ghost pipe from the ground. It was translucent and reminded me of the spirit friends I'd made. Of the knowledge I now held that their presence was guarded by an archdemoness. She kept them happy in their afterlives. Where would Meg and Edith and Paul... Arthur and Clara and the others... go without her?

Six men she'd killed already.

As I reached for a black tulip, something cold and red dropped on my knuckle. And then a splatter on my cheek. When I moved back, something crashed into the bush, breaking the branches. Then another thump. At my feet, a dead rattlesnake. When I looked up in horror, a falcon cawed, diving for a viper curled to strike. I screamed, running toward the bird, only for the sun to be darkened by a flock of gray falcons. Blood rained from the sky as they issued their attack. Some fell prey to the death bites of the serpents curling between their talons who used their last moments to crash the bird to the ground with a screech of pain.

It was a war.

And then a scarier sound than any creature could emit rent the air. The cry of men behind me. Lord Harkness's men split into parties, some charging through the maze, some stomping through the deadly garden. Pollen erupted, and they gargled, coughing, and dropping to their knees, holding their throats as the blooms did their jobs in painfully sucking the life from them. But there weren't enough deadly flowers to stop the dozens of men holding swords and guns.

I ran toward the manor. I had to warn Lady Venom. We had to hide her. Edith floated by the door, her hands over her mouth to hide a sob. "You have to warn Lady Venom," I stumbled on the stairs. "Now!"

Nodding, she seemed to understand and charged through the door. I stopped, turning around to the carnage around me. Snakes lay dead in puddles of blood, intertwined with spread wings and feathers of falcons as more birds cawed above me and men shouted. A snake hissed down the stairs toward the commotion. Not running, not hiding. Everything here, from the animals to the flowers, was fighting for its home, for its lady. I ducked behind the stairs as men charged into the manor. Something fired, and they screamed before they quickly silenced. Peeking over the stone wall, I found Meg floating out, holding a bloodied candlestick holder. She spotted me and grabbed my shoulders. "Lady Venom has ordered me to conceal you. Come, let's go."

More men stormed past, and we ducked. One yelped in pain as a cobra struck his thigh. "This is my home, too," I breathed. "I'm not running."

Meg grinned. "I was hoping you'd say that." She reached behind her back and handed me the ebony box I'd used for practice. My gift from my lady in so many ways. It was time to repay her.

I took my knives and strapped them to my body, holding two in my hands and fastening the round, curved and hooked knives to my side. "Let's kill some men," I murmured.

I stepped out from the stairs, garnering the attention of two men, who pointed and hollered. "There she is! Grab Lord Harkness's wife!"

They stormed toward me, and I put my fingers between my teeth and whistled, knowing who'd come for me. The men each grabbed one of my arms, not seeing the knives I clutched, because when you hold them right, you can't see them. "I'm no man's wife," I corrected. They didn't expect me to be strong or to fight back. So when I twisted my wrists and slid the blades through their jugulars, the looks of shock on their dying faces was priceless. I smiled in triumph as they dropped to the ground. Just then, my horse, Penny, galloped next to me in a flash of white. "Come on, Penny. To our lady."

I kicked her sides, and she stormed past the battle of scales and talons, venom dripping and birds screaming, while men writhed their shocks of slow venom and flower poison. The snakes were winning, but barely, and more men were coming. A lethal chorus of rattles, swift strikes, birds crying, and men dying sang through the air.

Penny bounded up the stairs, and I pulled her mane, directing her toward the west wing. The ghosts turned to things of nightmares. No longer were they friendly spirits brewing tea and sharing secrets. They transformed into shadowy black creatures that sent chills down my spine. I gasped as two split a man in half, his blood pouring onto the hardwood floor. It was the stuff of nightmares... and I was on their team. I was one of them now, the blood from splatters of battle and the blunt edge of my knives reddening Penny's white coat.

We made it to Lady Venom's room, and I barreled through the doorway, startling at what I found.

"There she is. Coming back to me like the errant wife she is," Lord Harkness growled.

He held Lady Venom by the throat, a horse whip tied tightly around her delicate neck. And she stood, one man dead already on the floor. Seven men dead.

And if she killed Lord Harkness, she would die. She'd be tortured in hell, and the ghosts would be gone forever. One wrong move, and he would win.

This would all go away.

And I was good as dead without my lady.

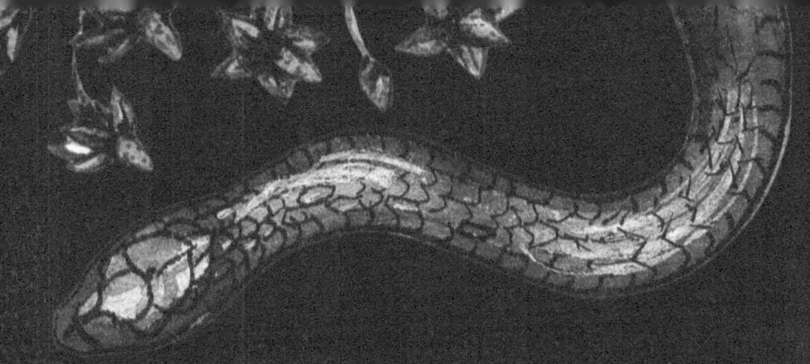

CHAPTER TWENTY

I PUT MY PALMS up. "Release her. I'm what you want. I'll go with you. Marry you. Just let her go."

Lady Venom's jaw was tense as she stood under his hold. He didn't deserve to lay a hand on her, and I fantasized and plotted how I could cut that hand off in that moment. Her furrowed brows only met my gaze. What were we going to do?

"She's sullied you. Bewitched you," he spat. "Damaged property. That's what you are, Poesy. Though your disobedience will be punished publicly for the scene you've caused. Go with my men while I have my way with your captor." He shoved his nose to her ear. "Not so strong, not so lethal now that a real man has found you, are you?"

My hand inched toward my throwing stars. I'd never made this shot before. Every scarecrow in front sliced along with the one behind it. I couldn't risk harming her with a poor throw.

Lady Venom's voice was steady when she spoke with the authority of a queen. He was so much bigger than her, but she was twenty times the force he was. "The manor is nothing if you kill me, and you know as well as I that Poesy is not the bride you seek. So take me, my power. I will be yours to wield, to use and abuse as you see fit. Only... leave her be. No man will touch her, and no bids will ever be placed on her again."

"No!" I yelled.

Lord Harkness scoffed and loosened his hold slightly. "Poesy, you do know that your lady here started the biddings, don't you? I did my homework, studied up like I would before any hunt. Fascinating what I found."

"What?" I asked in shock.

Lady venom swallowed, looking down. "I would dress my friends up and have the boys pick the prettiest costumed girl and lead them around in ribbon. The men liked the idea and began it for real." She glared at the lord. "My friends hated me after—rightly so—and I ran into the woods, distraught and outcast. I came upon a traveling man outside the gates of the manor." She rattled a sigh. "He asked what I would trade to be the lady of the haunted manor. I said anything. He said *your body*. I said *yes*."

Lord Harkness interrupted roughly. "He was a devil, and he cursed her. Saying you will live forever as lady of the manor, but you can only kill seven men a year. No more. And you must kill seven men a year. No less. You are to look after wayward spirits. To give you something to live for and a chance to atone for your actions. If a woman falls in love with you, the seven-man curse will be gone, and you can live freely."

Lady Venom looked to me and nodded. "It seems your lord has done his research in your absence." My mind whirled, the pieces all coming together.

Lord Harkness growled, rubbing his chin. "However, you propose an interesting prospect. You would have to agree to submit to me fully, so I'm known as the man who conquered the whore on the hill, broke her, made her his trophy. It's intriguing indeed. But I'll need you to prove your devotion here and now."

He grabbed her hair roughly and threw her to the ground. The sight broke me in half, and I let out a muffled sob. "On your knees," he ordered her, unzipping his pants.

She could have killed him there. It would have killed her too, but I know that wasn't why she didn't. He'd send his men, and I'd be unprotected and alone and punished. Lady Venom chose a fate worse than death, a stripping down of who she was, a quietening of her power and prowess. Instead of gutting Lord Harkness like the pig he was, she dropped to her knees before him while he pulled out his cock. My beautiful, perfect, strong woman would do anything for me. Give up all that she had and was to protect me. She'd take orders, a queen obeying a rat. And I had to save her. Had to find a way to get us out of this.

With a sly glance over her shoulder, she opened her mouth and raised a sultry hand, placing it on the lord's sternum and circling lightly. It dawned on me then. An invitation. She trusted me to make the shot.

He groaned a disgusting sound and closed his eyes, dropping his weapon and the whip the moment her lips touched him. It was my moment, and my fury made my hand tremble as I took out my throwing knife and reared back, remembering the way she'd coached me, remembering how she'd given me my knives, my voice, my power.

With the hardest force I could muster, I released the blade, and it spun through the air, hitting its target with a wet thud. He screamed, hands covering his bloody chest and jaw locking as his eyes widened. He dropped to his knees, and Lady Venom stood, passing me an approving smile before addressing him. She kicked him over and stood on his chest with her boot, intensifying the bleeding.

Taking a thumb, she touched his blood and licked it with her snake tongue as his eyes widened in horror at her demon. "Your blood tastes even worse than your disgusting cock. And now, both will die along with you. Your filthy dick will cause no more harm, and your bloodline dies with you. Know that I will enjoy fucking your fiancé on your shallow grave, Lord Harkness."

With that, she left him to shake in his slow death, venom from my blade foaming his mouth. I fell into her arms then, sobbing. "I'm so sorry," I cried.

"Shh," she coaxed. "I'm so proud of you, bellflower. You did so well."

I looked up at her glassy eyes, "I love—"

Suddenly, something pulled my hair backward, and I fell. One of the lord's men had crept in and thrown me to the ground. He lunged for Lady Venom, and with a spin, she grabbed the lord's sword and impaled him. "No!" I yelled, tears streaking my face. "Eight, that's eight!"

The man dropped to the ground, and Lady Venom's teary gaze found mine. "I suppose this is goodbye, my sweet foxglove. Look after the snakes for me?"

Her body began to fade, and I crawled forward, holding on to the hem of her silken black robe. "No," I bellowed. "No, you can't leave. I won't let hell take you. Do you hear that, devils? She's not yours. She's mine. I love her. I love you," I held her tight, as if I had the strength to keep the claws of the devil off her.

All of a sudden, the fading stopped, and she was solid again. And somehow, the sky brightened, and the cawing of falcons ceased.

When I looked up, Lady Venom was smiling and rubbing my hair. "I love you, too. Look at you, little curse-breaker. Now, I can live and kill. Now the biddings will end, because you were captured and learned to love a monster."

In the doorway, the ghosts congregated. "A mistress to love and be loved." Edith clutched a hand to her chest. "The battle is won. The bargain fulfilled. We are safe now."

"So, I did something right?" I wiped my tears. "No hell?"

"No hell," Lady Venom purred. "Only the one we create here together. My love, my wife."

"Wife," I breathed. "Yes."

That she was, and that I was to her. To hell and back until the ends of time. A mistress to fulfill a devil's bargain and a lady to curse a girl forever.

CHAPTER TWENTY-ONE

Six Months Later

My shovel pierced the earth under the grove of cherry trees and filled the skull with dirt as my wife patted ghost pipe into its new planter. "Lord Harkness's big head was finally good for something after all," she mused, taking a cherry between her teeth and biting.

"I'd like a taste, too," I said, pushing the skull of my dead fiancé out of the way and crawling toward her. She put a cherry in my mouth, and I grinned. "A different kind of cherry." My hands pushed up her skirts, and she lay back in the soft spring grass.

"As you wish, my love," she conceded, opening her legs for me. "I am ready for you."

I gasped at the sight of her perfect and bare pussy. "No undergarments? My naughty, naughty lady..." I breathed, dipping between her thighs. I extended my forked snake tongue and flicked it against her clit. "But I suppose it's an offering fit for the demon I now am."

She leaned up on her elbows. "And demoness looks so good on you."

A consequence of robbing hell of an archdemon was to transform into one as well. But I didn't mind. In fact, my lady and I were overjoyed that I would now live forever with her. In our manor, with our ghosts, our snakes, and our knives... killing as many men as we wished. It was a dream, a nightmare, made for two.

I pushed my tongue inside her, and she sighed, letting the taste of her love and dark devotion mix with the cherry taste of her sex. I lapped at her core and pushed my fingers inside until she broke into bliss around my mouth and knuckles. Her surrender was so sweet. Tasting her was the most delicious dessert. A cherry pie all my own. As her breathing slowed from her third release, I looked up, licking my lips. "You asked me, when I came here, whether I was brave or stupid."

She shot me a wicked and sharp-toothed smile. "I remember."

"Well, my love, I am both. Brave and lethal, and stupid and hopelessly enamored with you, Lady Venom."

She sat up and cupped my face. "And you, my dear bellflower, are my captive, my mistress for the rest of time. And I will never, ever, set you free."

I never wanted to be free of her. My monster, my archdemoness. It would be the two of us and our snakes and horrors forever.

And they lived dreadfully ever after.

For all the girls like me who grew up needing to see the duality and fierce beauty within lesbian love.

Thank you to my readers for supporting this sapphic tale. This story came to me in a dream, and I woke up with a tremendous need to write it, though I was right in the middle of writing a very different series. I shared the dream on my Tiktok, of the girl stumbling through the snake-filled maze and falling into a woman's arms and that woman asking who she needed to kill. That was the dream, the scene, that started it all.

And reader Boo Hallows was one of the first to excitedly champion my reckless abandon in creating it. Meg, who had a ghost named after her, is the kindest champion of indie authors and all things loving and strange. Sav, my friend and PA had been begging for another sapphic read from me forever, and encouraged the idea. And my best friend and fellow author Dakota Wilde, who would support anything I did but would never let me get bangs, assured me the idea wasn't just good but necessary.

And that's how the whole passion project of writing this has felt. Like something needed and necessary to launch into the realms. I think lesbian romance should be featured in every genre, but I could think of no better to start with, for me, than something gothic and haunted.

So thank you again for picking this up and wandering into the woods with Poesy. Stay tuned for more sapphic love in the thorneverse.

Haunt me

• Sign up for my newsletter to be the first to know about new book releases

• Join my patreon for NSFW art, early chapters of The Halloween Boys, secret projects, and more.

• Join me on #spicybooktok TikTok: @katblackthorne

• See fan edits on Instagram @katblackthorneauthor

• Follow for updates and quotes on Twitter: @blackthornekat

• Follow me on Amazon for upcoming books:

• Join my reader coven on FB Kat Blackthorne and the Black Hearts Coven

Business or press inquiries please email katblackthorneauthor@gmail.com

Also by Kat Blackthorne

The Halloween Boys Series
(Meet Ezmerelda here)

Ghost

Dragon

Wolf

Devil

Wicked Ecstasy

Come For a Spell

Familiar Taste